**W**e stopped at the gate and Art turned toward me, his hand moving to the back of my head. We started to kiss. We were used to each other now. I loved the way I was beginning to know his mouth, its responses, its taste. He was working his fingers into my hair. His other hand moved from my neck. Then after a while it moved lower, across my stomach. I was trembling, a bit. All the times I'd thought about it, and now it was happening. Without quite meaning to, I pulled back slightly.

"You're shaking," he said. "You can't be cold."

"I'm not," I whispered.

We started kissing again. This time I didn't pull back.

ALSO BY
KATE CANN:

SEX
GO!

# Ready?

### Kate Cann

HarperCollins*Publishers*

Ready?

Copyright © 1996 by Kate Cann

All rights reserved. No part of this book may be used or
reproduced in any manner whatsoever without written permission
except in the case of brief quotations embodied in critical articles
and reviews. Printed in the United States of America.
For information address HarperCollins Children's Books, a division
of HarperCollins Publishers, 1350 Avenue of the Americas,
New York, NY 10019.

First published by Livewire Books, The Women's Press Ltd, 1996,
A Member of the Namara Group, 34 Great Sutton Street, London
EC1V 0DX

Library of Congress Cataloging-in-Publication Data
Cann, Kate.
[Diving in]
  Ready?/Kate Cann.
      p.     cm.
Sequel: Sex.
Summary: Intrigued by a gorgeous boy she sees at the swimming
pool, sixteen-year-old Coll begins a relationship with him and is
dismayed to find him both more experienced and more forceful
than she is.
    ISBN 0-06-440869-8 (pbk.)—ISBN 0-06-028938-4 (lib. bdg.)
    [1. Love—Fiction.   2. England—Fiction.]   I. Title
PZ7.C169 Re   2001                                     00-059698
[Fic]—dc21                                                  CIP
                                                             AC

Typography by Henrietta Stern
❖
First HarperTempest edition, 2001

Visit us on the World Wide Web!
www.harperteen.com

TO JEFF

# No. 1

As the hot water pounded down on me, I was suddenly aware I was not alone. Someone was standing very close to me, under the same shower. I opened my eyes, blinking away water. It was him. He must have followed me out of the pool. Water was splashing onto his broad shoulders, running off his body and onto mine.

He shrugged, smiled. He was so beautiful. "All the others are taken. Do you mind . . . sharing?"

I couldn't answer. Without knowing what I was doing, I began unscrewing the cap from my shower gel.

He took it from me. "Let me do your back. The bits you can't . . . reach." Then he turned me round gently and began rubbing gel over my shoulders, with wonderful, sensual strokes . . .

"You've got fabulous skin," he murmured.

I turned slowly toward him under the pounding water. His face was almost touching mine. He laid one hand against my cheek, and said . . .

"ARE YOU DEAD OR JUST COMATOSE?"

1

My mind twitched. Winced.

"Colette! Can you HEAR me? I've been shouting for hours! Have you died up there or something?! Shift yourself! If you intend EATING dinner tonight perhaps you could come and put some MINIMAL EFFORT into its CREATION!"

And with those words my favorite fantasy was nuked. The steamy shared shower evaporated. My grim, solitary bedroom took its place.

Reality was back.

It was my mum shouting. She likes to use words, lots of them. "Come and help get dinner" is far too homely a phrase for her. And she likes to be loud. Very loud.

With a groan of regret I heaved myself up from my bed. I hate the way Mum blasts into my inner life like that—just as it'd been getting really good, too. It's bad enough sharing a living space, but when you have your fantasies invaded as well it's too much. Mind you, it was a pretty pathetic fantasy. A total fantasy. Guys like the one I was thinking of didn't come and share your shower at the pool. They hung around glowering until one was free, or they kicked someone younger and weaker out of theirs.

I trooped downstairs, deflated. Cooking sounds and smells met me halfway down. Thursday night suppertime. Exactly the same as all the other suppertimes. They were supposed to be the high point of the day, the warm center of our shared family existence. I hated them.

Every member of the family was expected to help prepare the meal, or Mum lectured you on freeloading. She was very hot on not being a domestic slave. She said that would be deeply unhealthy for all of us, not just her. I thought it might have been quite nice sometimes—kind of restful—but I suppose I could see her point.

The kitchen was in its usual chaos—never quite cleared up from the last meal, every surface crammed with stuff. Mum was standing at the stove, banging away theatrically and cooking up a big pot of her special Mediterranean stew. She dominated the kitchen. Dominated it? She practically filled it.

"Larger than life" is how her admiring female friends describe her. You couldn't describe her as fat, that's too lazy a word. Enormous will do. She has formidable energy. She's strong. She's loud. And she's *huge*. "Disagree with me," she seems to say, "and I'll crush you!"

My little sister Sarah was in the kitchen, too, standing at the table. She would have already peeled the potatoes, mixed the crumble, earned Mum's approval. She makes a religion out of Being Helpful. Evil little creep.

Mum turned from the stove to glare at me. "Ah, Colette, you've decided to JOIN us at last, have you?" she boomed. "Very good of you. Perhaps you could chop some cucumber—if that's not too ONEROUS a task?"

Dad came through the door. He must have heard

3

Mum bellowing. Come to think of it, they must have heard her five doors down the street. He looked anxiously toward the stove and asked, "Anything still to do, dear?"

Mum picked up the colander of draining potatoes and shook it furiously, as though she'd caught it stealing from her handbag. "No, Frank. As usual, it's all in hand."

Dad gave a little shudder. He had Failed To Help—again.

Sharing the housework was the subject of an ongoing, bitter dialogue between my parents. Well, more like a one-way complaint from Mum to Dad. It's sad, because Dad genuinely believes that men and women should share the work in the house, but somehow he never manages it. He gets so involved in his own work—he's a freelance architect—that it's always too late by the time he offers any help. So all Mum's views about the worthlessness of men are confirmed, and she's permanently resentful, pointedly martyred.

She has a job, too, you see, five mornings a week. Speech therapy. That's a joke. She'd be the only one doing the speaking. Her patients must need therapy when they LEAVE one of her sessions. It must be pretty tense being locked up with her for an hour, trying to get a word in.

Mum spooned a large dollop of stew into her mouth, savored it, and announced that supper was ready. Dad sat down guiltily and I joined him. Mum heaved the huge cast-iron pot from the stove and slammed it on the table. Sarah followed virtuously with the potatoes. Supper—oh, joy—was served.

"Well, Sarah," Mum beamed as she doled out plates of red and green gunk. "How was your GYMNASTIC SESSION today?"

We were on to Stage Two of the family meal. The bonding. The sharing. The sitting-down-as-a-proper-family. No matter if you wanted to go out, or had belly-ache and couldn't swallow a thing—you sat down As A Family and talked together. Correction. Listened to Mum together.

I switched off. First my mind drifted back to my swimming-pool fantasy, but that was a bit uncomfortable, with Mum and Dad sitting right across the table. Sex, you understand, had no place in our homelife. It was absent, acknowledged only in theory. We were the family of Immaculate Perception. In fact I still couldn't quite believe that Mum and Dad must have done it nine years ago, to get Sarah. Maybe they'd just found her under a gooseberry bush, like the old stories said. Or by the drain, or something.

So I switched safely to thinking just about swimming. I always go swimming on a Thursday night, and I really enjoy it. That great pure rush of water as you dive in, washing all the clatter of the day away. The silence under water. That feeling of power as you move forward, faster and faster.

And—getting back to sex for just a minute—tonight, Achilles might be at the pool. On a Thursday, he nearly always was.

Achilles is the subject of all my endless fantasies. I've been watching him for weeks now, and dreaming about him. It makes my real life a bit more bearable.

He's a great subject for a fantasy, too. He must be about seventeen and he's *gorgeous*. Long, lean, muscular. Thick, dark brown hair. And there's something about his face that just—well, I fancy him so much it hurts. It gives me a real, physical pain sometimes.

He swims very fast, no splashing, like a shark. He gets out of the pool very fast, too—you have to be quick to see him go. I started calling him Achilles because he makes me think of a Greek god—and because he has an A monogrammed on his very posh towel. It probably stands for Andrew or something, but I think of him as Achilles. Exquisite, heroic—

"RHUBARB CRUMBLE, Colette—or is that too prosaic for your refined tastes?" Mum's voice interrupted my blissful thoughts. Again. She must somehow tap into my mind processes and step in to censor them whenever they get near sex.

I mumbled something about needing to get to the pool, then I shot off to get my bike, high on the thought that I might see Achilles. Pathetic? Well, everyone needs something to look forward to in their life.

# NO. 2

**O**n the road, I pedaled fast. I needed to work off some of that Mediterranean Stew before I got in the pool. The roads were crawling with the usual bike-blind motorists, but I managed to get to the sports center in one piece. As I freewheeled in, the carpark was filling up with the executive bunch arriving for their after-work anti-stress exercise sessions. I locked up my bike and headed through the big glass doors. I seemed to be the only person there under thirty.

The sports center is very flash. It closed down last winter for refurbishment. When it reopened in the spring the prices had been refurbished, too. Now lots of kids from the town just can't afford to go anymore. Mum is loud in her condemnation. Local needs, she says, have been betrayed, and commercial concerns have been allowed to rule. The old pool has been turned into an elitist health club.

In theory I agree with her, but in practice I have to admit I love the new place. It's light and airy with hot open showers and huge tropical plants. It's a treat just to go there.

Despite her misgivings, Mum paid for my membership so I can swim there as often as I like. She only feels the need to tell me how privileged I am about once a week or so. There was one condition attached to her generosity—that I also do self-defense classes at the same place. You get a special reduced rate for them if you're a member. Mum wants me well equipped for the male-female war ahead.

I found a cubicle and changed, then I stopped in front of the mirrors to tie back my hair. My reflection never exactly cheers me up, but at least my hair's OK. It's long and dark and I've got masses of it. After my eyes, which are also kind of long and dark, it's probably my best feature. Not that you see much of it, tied back for swimming.

I went out to the pool, dived in, and swam the first length slowly, to warm up. Then I looked around me, hopefully. I was rewarded. Achilles was walking out of the changing rooms. He moved easily, with just a trace of male swagger.

I pulled up at the side, pretending water had gone up my nose so I could stare at him. "You creep, Coll," I scolded myself. "You besotted creep." But I stayed watching.

He walked to the edge of the pool, looking down its length to find a space to swim in. Long legs, broad shoulders. And that face. I ogled shamelessly. He moved a couple of steps to his left, and pulled on his goggles, obscuring—though not completely—his gorgeousness. Then he dived into the water with barely a splash.

I took a deep breath. I realized I was grinning. "You lech," I said to myself. "You lecherous cow."

But I felt wonderful. Just to see him felt wonderful. I shot under the water and plowed up to the deep end, first crawl, then breaststroke. I was only two lanes away from him. Length after length after length. Swimming along in the same water as him, washed over by his waves. Smitten.

One day, I told myself, I'm going to speak to him. Just not yet. He might ignore me, snub me, laugh at me. Fantasy was safer.

All I really managed to see of his face as we swam was a quick blur as he swung round at the end of the pool. Then, as I came to the end of my thirty lengths, I couldn't see him at all. He must have done his usual top-speed exit.

I heaved myself out of the water, disappointed. The buzz had worn off a bit. In fact I was exhausted. I stomped off to the poolside showers and took my time shampooing my hair and rinsing off the chlorine. There were half-a-dozen other people sluicing off with me and their "yaah—oh, absolutely" conversations were excruciating to listen to. One guy obviously felt acutely deprived not having his mobile under the shower with him. He kept yapping away about having to touch base with Geoffrey on the latest figures soonest. Enough to make you puke.

Grumpily, I left the showers, headed toward the lockers—and ran smack into Achilles.

I rebounded backward. *"S-ss-sorry!"* I breathed. I sounded like a deflating balloon. I bet I looked like one, too—a big pink one. I felt myself glow with shock, embarrassment, and the fact that for one second at least I'd been in head to toe contact with him.

"I've made you wet," I said, reddening further.

He laughed, briefly. "Not much. You OK?"

What a *voice*. Deep. Intelligent. Fabulous.

I have a thing about voices. I once trailed a gorgeous-looking bloke for weeks, in and out of Wimpy bars, through the shopping center and up to the park, only to find that when he spoke he sounded like a chipmunk. My lust had died with the discovery.

"F-fine," I stuttered. "S-s-sorry." Wow, I'm some conversationalist.

He smiled. White teeth, stunning. Damp hair clinging to his forehead. My knees buckled slightly. Then he walked off.

The bike ride home was to the sound of Beethoven's Fifth in my head. As I pedaled I occasionally shot out a hand to conduct the really powerful bits. He had spoken to me. *He* had spoken to *me*.

Not even getting home that evening could dampen my spirits completely. "Anyone around?" I shouted cheerfully, as I let myself in.

"Kitchen!" came the slightly surprised, slightly sarcastic reply.

Mum was still ensconced at the head of the big kitchen table but this time she had Claire, one of her friends, listening to her instead of her family. Dad and Sarah had scarpered. No one sits in on one of Mum's sessions with a friend unless they have to.

The sink was piled high with sticky-looking pans and a J-cloth had expired beside a trail of stew on the stove. The family clearing-up had obviously not happened. The pans would sit there for hours, dried food hardening like a reproach. Judging by the newly opened bottle of red wine on the table, Mum wasn't about to get up and start in on them.

Only me left. I was still feeling good enough to head for the sink intending to start scrubbing when Mum interrupted me.

"Colette!" she boomed. "Leave that, dear—do it later. Have some wine with us—get yourself a glass."

I wasn't sure which had the least appeal—washing pans or joining the twosome at the table. But I didn't really have a lot of choice. I got a glass from the cupboard.

Mum was holding forth on her all-time favorite topic—the inadequacies of the male sex. She

11

disapproves of men as a species. She thinks they're generally hopeless, worthless, and a complete waste of space. Not to mention destructive and violent and bullying. Not to her, of course—you'd need to be the Incredible Hulk before you pushed her around—but to most women. She thinks we'd be far better off in a single-sex world. Female-sex, that is.

I sat down with them and Claire smirkingly poured me out a couple of inches of wine. The conversation was focusing on Claire's ex now: he was getting a real drubbing. They carried on as if I was only a minor interruption. Which I suppose I was.

Mum liked me to sit in on these sort of conversations, especially now that I've turned sixteen. Learning from real life, real pain. Her many women friends—divorced, separated, or living, like her, in uneasy truce—were welcome to drop in at any time; open house. I called them the Wailing Sisterhood—to myself, that is. Some of them I liked, but most of them were awful, and they were so depressing to listen to. As far as they were concerned, men and women just couldn't get along, heterosexuality didn't work, and men, without exception, were pigs.

But I like men. I really do. I like watching them, thinking about them. I even hope to have one of my own one day. Sometimes when they all talk I feel like shouting, "So your life went wrong—why assume mine will? Maybe it'll work for me!" But this would only invite a pitying smile, and a "She'll learn" comment. You can't win with them. You can't even compete.

I took a last glug of wine and got up from the table. "Night, Mum," I said. "Night, Claire." They didn't really spot that I was leaving. At least I'd got out of the washing-up. If it was still there tomorrow morning, a symbol of the family that failed to share the chores, maybe I'd do it then.

In my room, I stripped off my clothes and rubbed some body lotion into my legs. I still smelled strongly of chlorine, despite the shower. Then I slid into bed.

As I shut my eyes, I let the smell of chlorine take me back to the pool. That impact when I'd bumped into him. His face close up. His perfect dive into the water. His voice . . .

# NO. 3

Friday morning. The alarm shrieks, Mum shrieks, Sarah shrieks, the cat shrieks. Only Dad, as always, is silent. I dress, have breakfast, and clear out.

School is a drag. It's all-girls. Mum's idea, of course. She'd read loads of statistics about girls doing better at single-sex schools, and this fed right into her prejudices. By the time she'd finished looking into it, she had the boys permanently rioting in class, while somehow at the same time monopolizing the teacher's attention, dominating class discussions, and electrocuting any female who tried to get near the computers. While the girls simpered at the back and did their nails.

"You're there to WORK," she'd announced to me. "Plenty of time for the other stuff later." Although her expression made it clear that she'd prefer it if I never got round to the "other stuff" at all.

"In an ideal world," she'd said, "of course you'd learn alongside boys. Things would be equal. But we are very far from an ideal world, Colette. And your education comes first."

After my GCSEs, I'd really wanted to go on to our local sixth-form college, where you don't have to wear a uniform and the other half of the human race is let in through the doors. I'd put up quite a fight. But Mum fought back even harder, and in the end it was easier to get swept along by her terrible energy, and swept back in to St. Catherine's for the next two years.

I've got a best mate there, at any rate. Her name's Val, and she's mostly OK. She's redheaded, Irish, funny. We discuss everything together. As I staggered through the gates, my leg muscles still aching from last night's thirty lengths of extra-fast swimming, we met up as usual and kind of groaned together in greeting.

"Get that work done you were worried about?" I asked her. It was an essay on William Golding she hadn't been sure how to tackle. She'd cracked it, of course. There are two things Val does well. Work and eat. Not necessarily in that order.

"So was he there, then?" she asked. "Your hunk? At the pool?"

"He was there," I breathed. "He spoke to me. I bumped into him."

"All *right!*" crowed Val. "What *happened?*"

"Well—that was it, really. I just said sorry."

"Ah."

"Oh, Val, you should *see* him. He's stunning; he's so fit. You should *see* the way he dives into the water. And his *mouth* . . . kind of full, and a great shape . . . He had a brown jumper on yesterday. It just looked so *good* with his browny-black hair . . ."

"Coll," Val finally interrupted, "You're going to have to take action. I can't stand listening to you bleat on about him much longer. No one could. Next time you see him, try one of your self-defense moves on him. Make out you thought he was attacking you and chuck him over your shoulder. That'll get him talking to you."

Sometimes she's not that funny. "He *has* talked to me," I said. "I know what his voice is like now—it's fabulous, it's . . ."

"Here we go," groaned Val.

". . . quite deep, and really sexy, and *intelligent* sounding, I mean, Val, I really think he's got a brain, he thinks about things, you know?"

Val's eyes were skyward. "Give me strength," she said. "If there is a God, Coll, you will end up with this guy. Because a loving God could not bear to see me suffer anymore listening to *all this crap!*"

"You don't mean that," I said. She didn't mean it.

The bell went. Somehow, inevitably, we got through the day. A good English session on *Jane Eyre*, a book I love but naturally pretend to be bored by. A terrible history lesson on the Cold War. Private study when I privately daydreamed. Then Friday afternoon netball. The gorgeous Sam and her gang stood around gossiping and shivering and dropping the ball. They started sniggering when I got my second goal and Sam called out, "Why don't you take up rugby, Coll? You've got the shoulders for it."

I ignored her. I'm not sure how I feel about my body. Sometimes I think it's great—it's strong, kind of definite, and when I'm swimming I love it. But if the measurement of how good a body you have is looking good in a little Top Shop frock, then Sam would win manicured-hands down.

Besides, it's a kind of creed with Val and I not to make a big deal out of how we look. It's your mind, your being, that counts, we tell each other. Tarting yourself up is just too tacky for words. We have moments of doubt, when it seems like all the best-looking males around love tackiness, but by and large we stick to it. Anyway, I don't think I could stand the comments from Mum if I started wearing lipstick.

"What'll we do tonight, then?" Val was saying, bouncing a ball right next to Sam, who moved off, cursing. "It's Friday. We've got to do *something.*"

We looked at each other in glum silence. Once again we were up against the great universal law of Friday night. You had to do something good, something exciting. But since there was rarely anything good or exciting on, we usually ended up sneaking into the pub and nursing half a lager all night, or if we were really broke,

17

really desperate—The Youth Center.

Only the sound of the bell saved me from complete depression. The day was over. "Well, I'm broke," I said, grumpily, as we walked off the playing field. "And there's nothing going on. See you at the Center?"

We arranged to meet up at eight.

# No. 4

When I got to the Center that night, I went straight to the café—not the most riveting of places. It's painted sludgy green with lots of posters around telling you not to do drugs or have unprotected sex. A nice homely lady serves out the Coke and coffee. She looks like the Pillsbury Doughboy's mum; you can't imagine anyone feeling like having any kind of sex, protected or not, under her floury eye.

Val was there already, with a couple of other people we knew. Everyone was looking a bit bored, wanting to be somewhere else.

Then I saw Greg arrive. He, I have to admit, is one of the better things about the place. He's our age, in our situation—he has a fierce father who made him go to our "brother" school, Wellingrave. He's not exactly good-looking, but he has a nice, squashy sort of face, full of expression, and these dark Marmite-pot eyes. He's funny, a bit silly. And he really likes me. We've been out a few times, but I've put the brakes on it ever becoming regular.

"I like you as a *friend*," I'd told him.

This stunningly unoriginal line did not please him. "You mean I'm a crap snogger," he'd said.

"Don't be daft," I'd answered. "It's not that. It's just—look, let's just keep it casual, OK? We can still go out sometimes—I'm just not getting all tied down, OK?"

So that's what we did. We went out sometimes, to a film or a club or a party. And we saw each other at the Center. We'd fallen into this kind of pattern. When we went on a date we had a snog at the end of the evening—when we were at the Center, we didn't. Unwritten rule—never broken.

And he wasn't crap at kissing, not really. It's just that I'd never really wanted to snog him in the first place. I liked talking to him, because he was clever and funny, but I didn't watch his mouth when he spoke and imagine plastering my lips on it. Not like Achilles. Snogging him would be . . . and I was off again. Fantasy land.

Warning: Fantasizing can seriously damage your health. It makes you deaf for a start. Val had to practically thrust her face into mine before I realized she'd been calling me over.

"We're over there," she said. "There—*look*—Greg and Rachel."

"I *saw* you, I *saw* you," I answered, "And I was coming over. I was just . . . thinking."

I followed Val over to join the group. Greg, as usual, was already center stage, making everyone laugh. He was describing some video his poor mum had got out the night before, all about King Arthur and the Knights of the Round Table.

"Jane's been doing Camelot at school, and Ma thought it would help her," he was saying. Jane's his little sister but a lot less poisonous than mine. "Ma wanted us to sit down as a happy family—she made quite a big deal of it. She even made a big pan of pop-corn.

"Anyway, the film starts and it's pretty violent. Lots of limbs being chopped off with axes. Dad's really get-ting into it, keeps saying 'what an accurate depiction of early warfare.' But then it starts getting a bit fruity. There's this wild feast scene at the castle and the Duke's wife does a dance for the warriors—sort of medieval stripper stuff. Dad's starting to look uncomfortable. Ma keeps handing him popcorn to distract him, hoping it'll go back to a nice bit of hacking and slaughtering soon."

We all laughed. Encouraged, Greg went on: "Anyway, then the King ends up having it off with the Duke's wife. *In full armor.* Seriously kinky stuff. Dad's nearly beside himself but he can't go over and turn it off or he'll look like an uptight prude. Next thing is Merlin comes to claim the baby this woman has. Despite being shagged by someone in a full-length metal condom, she's s'posed to have got pregnant. She's screaming as Merlin carries the baby off, and Ma leaps to her feet saying, 'Oh I can't *bear* this! I can't *bear* to think of any

21

poor woman having her baby taken away from her!'
and whacks the telly off. She trots out to make cocoa—
Dad disappears behind the paper. Great night."

We all laughed again. Then the laughter turned into
groaning. Family life. Who needs it?

"You know, your parents and Greg's parents should
do a swap," Val said to me. "I can just see your dad with
his mum. They could be *kind* to each other."

"Oh, sure," I said. "But what about the other two?
My mum and his dad? We'd be laying bets on who
carved up who first. Like putting a couple of rottweilers
in a cage together, and no food."

"Well, I'd back your mum," said Greg. "She'd rip
him *up*. He wouldn't stand a chance."

I pulled a face at him. But he was probably right.
The funny thing is, Mum really likes Greg. "Thank heavens
you're seeing someone who can do more than just
grunt, Colette!" she once pronounced. Greg makes her
laugh. And he helps clear the table and stuff. Maybe I'd
fancy him more if she liked him less.

A boy Greg knew wandered over and began chatting
to him. Val turned to me. "You know, it makes me sick,"
she said. "We're always talking about sex, even if it's
only in a film. But it's all just talk."

I shrugged. But she had a point. We *were* always
talking about it, in some form or other. Discussions,
jokes, gossip—but no real action. We were all still standing on the edge, scared to dive in.

22

I even had a little mantra to console me for still hanging onto my virginity—not that anyone had exactly battled to get it away from me yet. I read somewhere that strongly sexed people tend to have their first real sex later than others, not earlier. That's because it's important to them, and they want the time to be right. That was how I felt. I wanted the time to be right.

I didn't just want some basic physical interaction, either—I wanted total sex. Mind, body, feelings. I wanted to make love to another person in their entirety. You know—holistically. I didn't mind waiting. As long as it wasn't too long.

Greg materialized at my side. Maybe he sensed my thoughts. "Dave says there's a party on at Tom Sutherland's tomorrow night," he announced. "Well, not really a party. His folks are out and he can have a few friends in. Do you two fancy going?"

I looked at Val, and we shrugged, pleased. Yes, we'd go, we said. Then we all bought a can of Coke, watched some kids playing darts for a while, and mulled over the latest drug-pushing scandal at the Sixth-Form College. We arranged what time to meet tomorrow, said good-night, and drifted off home. It was only about 10:30.

Another wild Friday night full of passion and excitement. Not.

# NO. 5

On Saturday morning at ten to eight I came to in a state of rather bleary-eyed dreariness. By ten past eight, a bit more awake, I felt worse. Uh-oh, I thought. Depression attack. No single reason for it—just the feeling that I hated everything in my life. I get these fits occasionally. Nothing I do seems to get me out of them.

All the fizz of having Achilles say all of four words to me had fizzled out. In fact, I think it had added to my depression—the contrast between him and my non-event of a Friday night was so huge. It was also a downer that I'd let myself get so excited about it in the first place.

He Is Only Fantasy, my new miserable self intoned. It isn't going to happen with him, ever. Stop acting like a pathetic little kid, mooning over someone from afar. Time to grow up and realize life is usually dull.

That depressed me even more, of course. I was so down I even tried counting my blessings, which is what I used to do as a little girl when I felt bad. By half-past eight I'd only thought of two, and one of them I wasn't really sure about including. So I gave up and mooched downstairs. I pushed the cat off the kitchen table and sat down to eat some cereal. I didn't bother to wipe where the cat had been—the entire table looked so mucky, it didn't seem worth it.

Mind you, everything is kind of gray and mucky and smeary in our house. Mum doesn't believe in cleaning. To her, being houseproud is some kind of psychotic illness. In every room, floors crunch underfoot. The picture rails all have this layer of fluff on them, and the corners are like nature reserves for house bugs. ("Do not clean this corner! Colony of rare housemites breeding!") There's always piles of things everywhere, and underneath the piles, the furniture is dead and shabby.

Mum says our place looks lived in. It looks lived in all right—by a gang of tramps with Hoover phobia. She has this saying she keeps trotting out: "A clean house means a wasted life!" I suppose I can see what she means, but sometimes the state of the place really gets me down. Particularly when I'm down already.

When I'd finished breakfast I wandered out into the hall. I could hear Mum on the phone upstairs, haranguing one of her friends. Sarah was chasing the cat across the landing with a hairbrush, squeaking, "Come *on,* Sunflower sweetheart, you want to look *pretty* don't you?"

And I suddenly felt so weighed down by boredom

25

and depression that I had to sit down there and then on the stairs. I'll wither if I don't get away from this soon, I thought. From this never-ending sameness. I want *passion.* I want *change!*

Nothing ever changes in our house. It's like that weird old woman in that book by Dickens we had to study—Miss Havisham. Sitting there in her rotting wedding dress surrounded by piles of dust and cobwebs for years and years, time stopped. That was us, too. We certainly had the dust. Mum hadn't—sorry, no one had—cleaned up for weeks.

The rest of the day passed in a sort of gray fug. Mum glared at me as I slouched in for lunch and bellowed, "HORMONES again, I take it?" I hate it when she does that. As though my moods are totally on a chemical level, and therefore not worth discussing.

I met Val after lunch and we wandered round the shopping center. That in itself is a sign of despair, if you ask me. A sign of having absolutely nothing else going on in your life. Our shopping center is a kind of limbo place, a hell for the very, very boring on this earth.

"There must be *more,* Val," I said. "More than *this.* I mean, look at these people. They all look as though they've had their brains suctioned out through their earholes. All these shops, all this useless stuff that no one really needs. What are all these people here for?"

"Same as us, I suppose," she answered. "Nothing else to do."

"They're just here out of—out of *hopelessness*. Buying overpriced rubbish to fill the aching emptiness in their lives."

"Oh, don't start that again, Coll. You always do this when you're depressed."

"That doesn't make it any less true. In the absence of real meaning, people turn to possessions in a vain attempt to give their futile lives purpose." I'd once got halfway through a heavy book of Mum's called *Alienation in the Consumer Society,* so I knew what I was on about. "Obsession with outer appearance means an inner void," I continued.

But Val wouldn't play ball—she refused to answer me. We wandered in and out of Snob, then we decided we had just enough money for a Coke each and we sat down in one of those bijou little cafés that they position in among the shops. This one had awnings and strings of vegetables hanging from the walls. It was pretending to be Italian. Or was it French? It was completely phony, anyway, so it didn't really matter.

As we sat there in silence, making our drinks last, a couple came through the door. She was tall with short blond hair; he was a bit taller, brown-haired. They moved easily, with confidence. They must have been nineteen, twenty. Not at school, anyway. They had money—they were both carrying things they'd bought.

And they looked all right. However much I wanted to hate them, I had to admit they looked all right. They weren't doomed, vacant shoppers. They gave off this kind of happy aura.

"I bet they're in love," said Val, sadly.

I watched the girl, envy making my throat tight. She looked great, her clothes were good and everything, but she also looked as though looking great didn't take up most of her time. She looked as though she had plenty of time for other things—reading, walking, talking. Making love.

We watched them as they read the menu, laughing together over what they wanted. They made it look so easy, being happy like that. She pulled a top out of one of the carrier bags and held it up against her. He admired it, and then he leaned across, caught her hand, put it to his mouth, and kissed it.

I glanced over at Val. There was no need to say anything. We both knew what the other was feeling. Pretty soon afterward, we said "See you later" and went off home.

# N O. 6

**W**hen 7:30 came round that Saturday night I made myself change the sweatshirt I was wearing and run a brush through my hair. "While obsession with one's personal appearance is a sign of being a vacant prat, total oblivion to it is a sign of mental illness," I told myself.

Greg drove up to collect me at eight on the dot. Mum opened the door. "Good EVENING, Gregory," I heard her say in an approving and almost flirtatious fashion. It was nauseating. And she *always* calls him Gregory. I hate it.

They had a little chat about how his A levels were going. "Oh, shut up, you creep," I muttered, listening to his polite, cheerful voice as I slouched downstairs. What do you want to be nice to that old battle-ax for?

I had to listen to five more minutes of Greg sucking up to Mum before I managed to haul him out of the door and into his mum's Astra.

"What's up, Coll?" he asked, as we drove off.

"Nothing," I said. "Life."

"Have your folks been getting you down again?" he

said. "Your mum was on form tonight. Telling me her views on *Paradise Lost.*"

"Oh, great. What were they—that Eve should have kept quiet about the apple, ditched Adam, and gone it on her own?"

He laughed. "No—just some stuff about patriarchal symbolism."

"Oh, lucky *you.* Great start to a Saturday night."

"She's OK, your mum," he said, as we pulled up outside Val's. "At least she's got a brain." He put the brake on and then reached over to stroke my hair back from my face. "Come on, you miserable cow. Cheer up. Give us a smile."

"I don't feel like cheering up."

"OK, fine. Stay miserable. You look quite sweet when you pout like that."

"I am *not* pouting."

"Fine, OK. Your mouth always juts out like that. Here's Val."

Val got in and we drove on to pick up Rachel and Dave, then on to Tom Sutherland's. Everyone was laughing and joking in the car. Except me, of course.

The sort-of party came up to my low expectations. It was awful. Tom had a mum who wanted her son to have a social life, but worried about everything and planned meticulously against anything spontaneous ever happening. Not an ideal way to have a wild time. She and her husband had gone out but she'd left masses of instructions. Like—only eat in the kitchen and only use the downstairs bog. She'd got in pizza and put the oven on a timer so we *had* to have it at 9:30 sharp, when the buzzer went. She'd made "low alcohol" punch and put out napkins and little paper cups. She'd made a big effort and it felt as though her anxious presence was still in the house. It ruined any chance we had of enjoying ourselves. I felt really sorry for Tom in the end, especially when she phoned "to see how things were going" but not as sorry as I felt for myself.

I was a real misery. I sat hunched up on the floor clutching my paper cup and thought about the sort of Saturday night Achilles might be having. Beautiful women, intense conversations. People playing sax and dancing on tables and—*living.*

Tom's parents arrived back at 11 on the dot, and we all trooped out at 11:05. The five of us piled into Greg's car, and drove off. I was the last to be dropped off. Greg even stopped a few houses up the road. Oh, lord, I thought. This definitely counts as a date, then.

Greg turned the engine off, took my hand, and leaned toward me. I let him kiss me. After a while I started to kiss him back. What had I got to lose?

It made me feel even sadder, though. This was accepting what life had to offer. I was making do with second best because I didn't really fancy Greg. And he was having second best because my heart wasn't really in it. We were both shortchanged.

31

## NO. 7

By Sunday morning my depression was even worse. I have to do something drastic, I thought. The only things I could think of were slitting my wrists, or going swimming. I decided on swimming. I got out my stuff, got on my bike, and went.

I had no hope of seeing Achilles there. Not on a Sunday. He'd be doing something classy—Sunday lunch in a country pub, Sunday lunch with his girlfriend's family. Had it been possible to feel worse than I did, that thought would have done it.

The pool is always full on a Sunday, too. Dads take the kids while Mums cook the lunch. I surveyed the little bobbing heads without enthusiasm. Not a clear lane in sight.

Then I remembered the outdoor pool. They'd just opened it for what's laughingly called the summer season. Through the huge plate glass windows it looked freezing. But it was deserted apart from the lifeguard perched in his high chair, hunched miserably against the wind.

Squaring my shoulders, I marched outside. I ran up

to the edge, jumped in the air, caught my legs in a leg-tuck, and bombed into the pool. Ppplooooossh! Sheeeezzz! It was freezing, but great. I came up, spluttering and laughing.

About eight centimeters from Achilles' face.

I never really understood the meaning of embarrassment until that moment. It hit me with full force, like someone slamming a cricket bat into my stomach. I just hadn't seen him there. He'd been up against the edge, resting, and I'd launched myself into the air and practically landed on top of him, bum first. How it must have looked from his angle just didn't bear imagining. I wanted to die. To glide down the drainage slit with the leaves and drowned flies.

Instead, I said (again): "S-s-sorry!"

He was laughing. Just let me *die*, I thought.

"That's OK," he said. "You only splashed me. Not a bad way of getting into a freezing cold pool."

My raging embarrassment calmed down a bit. I laughed a bit, too.

"They're supposed to heat it but it's murderous," he went on. "Then when the weather gets hotter, you have to deal with all the little kids from inside. Can't win."

My admiration doubled on the spot. With a few words he'd absolved me of my prattish behavior. My face was still bright red, but that could have been the cold. It was difficult to function normally, though, face to face with my fantasy.

*Converse!* my inner voice told me. *Say something! Anything!*

"How long did it take you to warm up?" I asked. Not exactly Oscar Wilde, but it would do.

"Who's warmed up?" he said. "I'm still freezing. Come on. Let's put some lengths in."

And he was off. Of course, he may have just been dying to get away from this insane female who'd practically kamikazied him, but he sounded so companionable that I set off after him. Cold? What cold?

It was impossible to keep up with him, though, turbo-driven as I was, and after a while we got into a steady rhythm of passing and crossing, length after length. Suddenly he burst past me, doing the butterfly. What a show-off, I thought admiringly, as he plunged past. And what a back! All those muscles in all the right places! But a sudden attack of lechery can put you off your stroke, and I had to stop for a minute to cough out the water I'd swallowed.

I drew up at the deep end at around lap twenty and realized he was waiting there.

"You're some swimmer," he said. "I'm getting out now. I'm cold right through—aren't you frozen?"

Well, I was hardly going to say "Oooh, no. I'm fine thank you, I'll just stay and do my full thirty," was I? I nodded, shivered theatrically, and clambered out after him.

It was a bit odd. There we were, heading for the

showers together—only we weren't together. I couldn't think of a thing to say. He got his towel and a tube of all-in-one washing stuff out of his locker. I got my towel and hid my daft little sponge bag underneath it. Blood was pounding in my ears, not only exercise induced.

He turned on his shower and began lathering the gel from the tube all over him, then he just stood there, face up under the hot stream of water. I was quaking. I shut my eyes under the spray.

Suddenly I heard "See you, then," looked up, and saw him disappearing from view through the archway.

He'd deserted me! I shot into the changing rooms, got my clothes, found a cubicle, toweled dry, yanked my clothes on, and ripped a brush through my hair. Only I wasn't sure why I was rushing. What did I hope to achieve? Nothing had really happened. He'd just said a few words to me, swam next to me . . .

"He's far too gorgeous to look at you," said my let's-be-sensible-just-who-do-you-think-you-are self. "He's out of your league. Stick to your fantasies. It's a lot safer."

But another little voice had begun to speak somewhere in the depths of my head, and it was saying: "If he'd been an average bloke, you'd have thought he was after you. Showing off his style. Complimenting your swimming. Chatting you up."

"Yes, but, he didn't mean anything by it," countered my sensible self. "How could he? It was nothing. He's too special."

**35**

"So if he'd had spots and spindly legs it would be called chatting you up, but as he's gorgeous it's called nothing?" said the new little voice. "Go on—trust your instincts! What have you got to lose? Go after him!"

"For goodness sake you're going to make a complete *idiot* of yourself and you're going to get *hurt*," wailed the let's-be-sensible voice. But it was growing fainter. And the other voice, growing stronger, shouted: *"Go for it! Go for it!"*

I shot out of the cubicle. I could feel myself shaking. I can't cope with this, I said to myself, as I rushed through the lines of lockers to the mirrors—and there he was. With his back to me. Combing his hair. His eyes in the mirror meeting mine.

"Hi," I said. It took huge bravery to say that word.

"Hi," he said. "Want a coffee?"

## NO. 8

OK, for Cleopatra or Isolde or another one of the great lovers of history it might not have packed much verbal punch. For me it was the most fantastic invitation I'd ever had. I sat at the little Formica table in the sports center coffee bar and no candlelit tryst could have been better. This was living. This was . . . perfect.

He was standing at the counter ordering coffee. I let my besotted gaze travel all the way down his wonderful body then I told myself sternly that looks aren't everything. He has to have a mind, too—I suppose. You must communicate. And that sudden thought terrified me.

What if we had nothing to say to each other? Or he thought I was a jerk?

He turned round and walked toward me, carrying two cups.

Let him not be a member of the National Front, I prayed. Let him not spend all his time whamming the keyboard of computer games. Let him like me.

He put the coffee on the table and sat down. "I need

this," he said. "Talk about chilled meat."

"Yeah, I'm cold right through," I lied. I was beginning to sweat.

"Keeps you sane, though. I had to come today. Get last night out of my system."

"Why, what happened last night?" I asked, not at all sure that I wanted to hear.

"Oh, one of my old man's dinner parties. He made me sit in on it. Make up the numbers. It was bloody awful. Boring discussions about wine, theater, who's shagging who. Lots of noise as they all got tanked up."

I stared. It sounded exotic, alien. "It sounds a lot more fun than Saturday night round at my place," I ventured.

He laughed. "I hated it. Still, nowhere else to go." (Nowhere else to go? Him? Fantastic!) "And they were all too far gone to want any of the pudding Fran had made so I sat there bored out of my mind and ate most of it on my own." He rolled his eyes. "Nearly threw up. Still, even throwing up can be more fun than listening to my old man when he gets going."

I laughed. I loved the directness of his speech. The energy. The anger? And I loved just looking at his face. It was pretty difficult, trying to carry on a normal conversation. But I had a go.

"Who's Fran?" I asked.

"My stepmother," he said. "So what sort of a night did you have?"

"Oh—a non-starter of a party. I was home by eleven."

He laughed. "I didn't escape till two. At least you got a couple of hours on your own."

So he rated being alone. Was it possible that someone who looked that good had an inner life as well?

"Er . . . my name's Art," he went on, spreading his hands as though asking for mercy. "For Arthur . . . laugh and I'll strangle you! Dad chose it. His need to go against the flow is a disease. Still, could have been Justin. Or Neville. Or Tristan."

Then we both laughed. I told him my name and—miracle! He'd heard of Colette, the French Colette.

"That's that writer, isn't it?"

"Yes," I said. "That's why I got the name. Mum loves her. And she loves the way she lived."

"How was that?"

"Oh, very independently—creatively—she was a survivor. And she ended up with some man about twenty years younger than her!"

"Sounds good," he said. "She wrote some pretty sexy stuff, didn't she?" He looked at me across the table. The energy between us was beginning to crackle.

"Yes," I managed to answer. "Very French sexy."

"French sexy!" he said, laughing. "I like that."

I dived like a coward into my cup of coffee. He went on to ask me about school, friends. I asked him a few questions back. We talked about swimming. I told him I sometimes ran, too. He said he didn't like running much, preferred cycling. I told him why running was better than cycling. Gradually, I began to relax. We were getting on fine. Talking to him was like standing on the boundary of a huge, new, uncharted land—nothing certain, nothing known. But I was taking the first steps into that land . . . and all the time the energy was beating between us.

Then after a while I saw that the coffee cups were nearly empty. Our time was up. I tried to make myself ask him out but I seemed to have been struck dumb. Say something, I begged him silently. Ask me out!

Art looked at his watch. "Ergh," he said. "I'll be late for lunch. We're supposed to be going to my uncle's and I'll have to overdose on fun things like looking at my cousin's stamp collection."

He was going. He was just going to go.

Then as he stood up he said, "You're here most Thursdays, aren't you? See you then?"

"Sure," I managed to croak. "I'll be here."

The delightful meaning of what he'd just said trickled into my brain. He knew that I came here every Thursday. He'd been watching me, too.

# NO. 9

On Monday morning, as we went into class, a goggle-eyed Val was treated to a blow-by-blow account of what had happened. "This is amazing, Coll," she crowed. "I thought it was all a fantasy. In fact I wasn't completely sure he actually existed."

"He exists, all right," I said. "I just can't believe it all happened. I *can't believe* I sat there talking to him."

"And he asked you for a coffee in your grotty old tracksuit," she said dreamily, "with your hair in rattails."

"Yeah, well," I said. "I didn't look that bad. Anyway, I want to get a new swimsuit. I've got to look good on Thursday."

"'Got to look good?'" she squawked. "What about all that stuff you were coming out with on Saturday—the inner void of outward appearances and everything? Now you're tarting yourself up . . ."

"Val, it's a new swimming costume I'm after, not a low-cut dress."

"Nothing wrong with your old costume," snorted Val. "It looks *fine*."

"It's not fine. It's tatty. I've had it for *three years.* It's got lots of little holes in it where I've unpicked all my swimming badges."

Val snorted again, irritatingly. "First sniff of a half-decent male and all your principles fly out of the window and you start tarting yourself up . . ."

Suddenly I felt really angry with her. "Val, give me a break!" I practically yelled. "That was *then.* This is *now!* I don't *care* about all that stuff now! I just want to look *good.* I want him to *fancy me!* I want to get *off* with him! I'll do *anything!*"

Just about everyone in the class had turned round to look at me. The gorgeous Sam was sniggering in disbelief.

"Blimey, calm down," Val said. Then, in a resigned voice, she continued, "Well, have it your way, Coll. Let's go shopping tonight. Then I suppose it'll be a new haircut and nail polish next."

"Well, I do need to get my hair trimmed. But not before next Thursday."

"You see?" she replied in gloomy triumph. "You'll be going on a diet next. How to become a sad bimbo in ten easy stages."

"Oh, belt up, Val. It's just to give me confidence."

"And that's just the sort of thing a bimbo would say. You're beginning to sound like one, Coll. You really are."

But she came shopping with me. She was my best mate, after all, and best mates will forgive you most things. Even ideological lapses.

I suppose I was compromising my principles a bit, but I didn't care. This was different. The incredible had happened. I'd got off with Art—well, nearly—I'd talked with him. Beside that, any scruples about inner superficiality just fell away.

Val and I trailed round all the usual places and I tried on lots of costumes but they were all hopeless. They were either really fancy, and made you look like you probably couldn't swim, or they were very sporty and made you look as though swimming was all you had on your mind. I suppose I wanted something in between.

Finally we went into one of those exclusive little underwear and sportswear shops. The assistant looked at our school uniforms with disapproval, but she let me take a handful of costumes into the changing room. The third one I tried on made me stop and stare at my reflection. It made my legs look long. It made my waist look thin. It looked fabulous. It was just plain black, like my old one, but there was something about the cut that was magic.

I stepped outside the changing room curtains, to show Val. She was impressed despite herself. "You look like a workout queen," she breathed. "And if that's what you want to look like, I should get it."

I hadn't even checked what it cost, I was so excited by how it looked. Then I found the price tag, and nearly fainted. It was so expensive.

"*That*'s why it looks so good," said Val. "Rich people

**43**

aren't really good-looking, you know. They just spend a huge amount on their clothes."

I continued to stare dumbly at the tag. "I'm a tenner short," I said. "And I completely cleared out my savings account."

"Oh, go for it!" said Val. "I'll lend you the tenner. Go on—take it."

I didn't even begin to put up a show of reluctance. I snatched the money out of her hands, hugged her, and shot off to pay.

Back home, bedroom door locked, I put the swimsuit on again and preened in front of my old dressing-table mirror. It was wonderful. Transforming.

Three days to go.

# NO. 10

The waiting was appalling. I didn't even begin to tell myself to be sensible, not to hang everything on Thursday. I was obsessed. If Art didn't turn up at the pool, or turned up but ignored me, I was simply going to dive off the top board in the wrong direction, and put an end to my miserable existence.

And if he *did* turn up—well, somehow I was going to get my man. I actually thought of it like that, too. Getting my man. If she'd known, Mum would have put me up for adoption.

All I wanted to do was talk about him. By Wednesday morning Val had, for the sake of her sanity, put a ban on any further discussion. By Wednesday night I was getting the shakes. And then Thursday arrived.

I could hardly eat a thing at supper.

"You're not DIETING, are you?" Mum barked as I pushed a bit of carrot round my plate. She viewed that in the same way most mothers would see heroin-addiction.

"No, of course not. I'm just—I'm really not hungry," I replied. Leave me alone, will you, I thought.

"You need energy to swim on, Colette," she said sternly.

Energy? I had energy. I had so much of it I felt I might explode at any minute.

At seven o'clock, stomach in a double knot, I got ready to go. It was quite a warm evening so I put on cycling shorts with my favorite big T-shirt over the top. I did my hair in a thick, even plait at the back instead of my usual scragged-back-into-a-band style. I even put on a bit of healthy-looking lipgloss. Then I packed my bag with towel and costume, fingers shaking. "Grow *up*," I kept telling myself.

I got on my bike and wobbled off. My legs didn't seem to be working as well as usual. I was sweating with nerves as I walked into the Sports Center. In the changing room, my wonderful new costume just sort of slithered on to me. My face shone with terror.

I dumped my clothes in a locker. Let him be there, let him be there, I prayed.

"Coll—hi!"

I spun round. And came face-to-face with Mike, one of Greg's friends.

"Hi!" I replied croakily, as if I was about to die from tuberculosis.

"How are you? Great to see you! Are you on your way in?"

Any other time, I'd have been quite pleased to have bumped into Mike. He was OK—a bit gung ho, but OK. Tonight I just wanted him to evaporate.

"I . . . I can't," I said. "I mean . . . I'm not sure. Not yet . . . I have to . . . I'll probably . . ." and I motioned toward the Ladies. Luckily, he had an all-boys'-school terror of anything remotely gynecological.

"Oh, *right*," he said, as though the gibberish I'd come out with held some great, solemn meaning. "Well, I'll see you in there . . . maybe?"

I stayed in the bog for about five minutes, lurked in the corridor a bit longer to make sure Mike had really gone, then slunk out to the pool. My eyes went into laser drive as I scanned the place.

I could see Mike swimming at the far end, but no Art. I peered anxiously at the sides, the exit, the outside pool through the great glass windows. Nothing.

Disappointment got hold of me. He was usually here well by this time. I sat on the edge and dangled my legs in the water. How long should I wait, I wondered, before I gave up on him? This was torture. Any longer and I'd start to hate him out of sheer self-defense.

Suddenly I sensed a presence at my side, and turned round. A self-satisfied looking creep I'd never seen before smiled down at me. I felt like crying.

"Hi!" he said.

*"Sod off,"* I hissed. Then, hopelessly, I dived in the pool.

OK, I thought, as I plowed through the water, I give up. He isn't here. He isn't going to turn up. He's forgotten you even exist. I accept defeat. The punishment for wanting something too much is to be denied it. The punishment for aspiring too high is to plummet to the depths. The punishment for . . .

Someone grabbed my ankle.

*If it's that creep I'll* . . . I shot round, snarling.

The ankle-grabber ducked backward, laughing. Then he came up for air. It was Art.

Joy and relief burned through me. It was Art.

"Thank God it's you," he said. "Just as I grabbed you I thought I'd made a mistake and I was going to get an earful. You looked ready to land one on me yourself."

"I thought you were a creep who'd been trying to move in on me."

"That guy at the other end? I think you scared him off. What did you say to him? The poor sod looked completely flattened."

He'd seen it then. I felt quite pleased. Man-slayer Coll.

"Come on," he said. "Let's go outside. It's like a sauna in here."

Actually, it was pleasantly warm, but I wasn't going to argue the point. We walked wordlessly out to the open-air pool and dived in. I was delighted we were on ankle-grabbing terms but a little doubt was niggling me about the speed with which he'd wanted to get swimming. I hope he doesn't just see me as a swimming partner, I thought. Our relationship to date has, after all, consisted almost entirely of lengths.

"Coll? Oh, yes—she's great to train with. *Fancy* her? Are you kidding?"

At around length number twenty-two Art pulled up at the end. "How many more d'you want to do?" he said, when I'd surfaced beside him.

"Well," I began, "I usually do thirty, but . . ."

"Fine!" he said, and set off again.

Oh, shit, I thought, and followed him.

Eight more, and we got out. We were both panting. That weird feeling of double-gravity you get when you stop swimming hit me more strongly than usual. I felt great—spaced out. We walked inside and past the café, where a little kids' party was going on. They were all throwing chips and jelly at each other and falling off their chairs, while a woman strummed a guitar and tried to get them to sing along to "The Wheels on the Bus."

"Looks fun," I said, sarcastically.

"Let's give it a miss," Art replied. "Have you eaten?"

"No," I said. It was true. I'd been too nervous to do much more than gag on Mum's veg-and-butterbean crumble.

"Well, I've been paid to eat out tonight," he said. "Dad's away—Fran's having some of her friends round. She met me at the door with a ten quid note. Told me to go and get a pizza. I said make it twenty and I'd clear off."

"You did *what?*" I gasped. "Did she give it to you?"

"You bet she did. She'd pay anything not to have me around when she's got her mates in. Can't discuss the old man with his son there, can she? I might report back."

I was stunned. Mum would *never* pay me to get out of the way when her friends came round. Far more likely that I'd pay her to let me escape.

"Anyway," he was saying, "Twenty quid will feed two. I know this place that does great steak sandwiches."

"Sounds brilliant," I said. "If You're Happy and You Know It" was now filtering down from the café, accompanied by shrill, miserable screaming. "Maybe the average age of the clients there'll be over five."

He laughed. "Come on. Let's go."

# NO. 11

A few minutes later we were cycling down the road. I usually take it pretty slow when I've been swimming, but Art didn't; I pedaled furiously to keep up with him. As we whizzed along the main road I saw Sam and her sidekick Tricia sauntering along the pavement in all their gear. Then, to my horror, Art skidded to a halt in front of them. Oh, no, I thought, don't let him *know* them!

He turned round. He looked fantastic. White shirt, brown skin, broad shoulders. Hair all blown back. Sam and Tricia obviously thought so, too. They leered in his direction.

He hadn't even noticed them. "This place—it's round the back of the railway," he called out. "We'll get there a lot quicker if we cut over that wasteland there. Is your bike up to it?"

"Sure," I said. "Let's go."

Sam and Tricia had turned to stare at me. I swung my bike out after Art in as reckless a manner as I could manage. I didn't actually shout *Up yours, girls!* but I enjoyed it as much as if I had.

On to the wasteland we went, Art hurtling over murderous ruts of hard stony earth and negotiating piles of rusty metal like some speeded-up cartoon character. I gritted my teeth and followed. Show him you can do it, I told myself, although I think I could have plummeted into a ditch and I'm not sure he'd have noticed. He seemed to be intent on breaking some kind of speed-and-danger record. A couple more pot holes, a long lethal bit of crazed concrete, and, mercifully, we arrived.

It was worth the journey. Just the sort of seriously cool place I'd expected him to know about. Someone had converted one of the old disused Victorian railway arches into a little licensed café. Rough old tables were spilling out of the door into the open, packed with people laughing and eating. I could hear jazzy piano music from somewhere, and smell grilling steaks.

"There's a table there," Art said, pointing. "Grab it."

I grabbed it, and we squeezed onto the bench together, not quite touching. I was so aware of him sitting next to me it was like having a five bar heater directed at my side.

A waiter appeared almost immediately, and we ordered.

"So," Art began, "what else do you do—other than swim, I mean? And run. I remember you told me you ran."

"Oh, I like reading. I like the cinema."

"Did you see that weird film about . . ." And we were off. Off on a conversation in which the words weren't really the point. Somehow, I managed to get my mouth to move, and make some sort of sense when I talked, but it wasn't easy. And when he talked I sat enthralled. To be honest, he could have sat there and quoted from the Magna Carta and I would have been enthralled, but he was a bit more interesting than that. I just wanted to stare at him, watch the way his mouth moved. Because the real communication wasn't with words. It was beyond the words, beneath them. It was an energy exchange. It was so strong, I felt sure he was feeling what I was.

The steak sandwiches arrived and, after one beer, we swapped to orange juice to avoid wobbling suspiciously on the way home. I made him laugh describing the horrors of coexisting with Mum, and I had a good moan about how there was never enough to do in our town. Inside myself, I kind of skated over the fact that his dad ran an ad agency and was obviously loaded; also that Art went to a high-fee-paying school in the next town. I told myself I'd think about the implications of that later.

After a while it got hard to keep the conversation going. I knew the evening had to come to an end, and I already felt all the tension of how we'd say goodbye. So much hung on it. Would we—you know, get physical? Would we arrange anything, make a date?

Art must have been thinking the same kind of thing. "That new band Schroedinger are playing here next week," he said suddenly. "At Sidwells. They're going to be big."

Sidwells was a local pub that had a hall set aside for live music. It was great when you could afford it.

"Schroedinger?" I replied. "I really like them. They're brilliant." I hadn't actually heard of them before now, but that little detail wasn't going to stop me.

"Look," he said, rather quickly. "I . . . sort of know one of them. I could get us tickets—should be a great gig."

"Sure," I said, casually, while my blood thrummed loud enough to deafen me. "What time?"

"Eight. It starts around then. I'll meet you at the door, OK?"

It was done. We'd achieved it. It lay in the air between us, precious, luminous. We had a date.

After that, it was as though we were free to go. I pooled my money in with his twenty quid, and we had just enough to cover the bill plus a final cup of coffee each. Then we unlocked our bikes, and headed off. Bikes are lousy for getting off with people, I thought. No back seats.

"Just go a bit slower, this time, will you?" I shouted, as we reached the road. Art collapsed over his handle-bars and slowed to an exaggerated crawl. I overtook. Five minutes later, he'd overtaken me again.

We got through town, and when we reached the corner by the library I pulled into the curb and shouted to Art. He wheeled round sharply and drew up next to me, front wheel touching mine.

"This is my turning," I said. "I'm two roads on down there."

"OK," he said. "Well—see you Saturday then? You be there, OK?"

"Sure. Well—bye then. See you Saturday." I started to pull my bike back, ready to move on.

Then Art got hold of my retreating handlebars, leaned toward me, and kissed me on the mouth. It wasn't pushy, but it wasn't exactly hesitant, either. I was still clutching my bike with both hands, but I stopped maneuvering it back pretty smartly. He drew away and we looked at each other, and then he leaned forward again, moving his hand from my bike to the back of my neck, getting hold of my plait of hair. I felt a kind of shudder of pleasure when he did that. It was different.

Our second kiss was a lot more definite, and it lasted a lot longer. It was warm, exploring. Art still had hold of my hair, pulling my head back gently. I brought my hand up to his shoulder, touching him at last. We were still kissing, moving closer. His bike wheel began to press into my knee. Mine must have been doing the same to his. Cars whizzed past, giving the odd honk. Until, finally, we drew apart.

"We're getting our spokes tangled," he said, and I

laughed. So you can get off with someone on a bike, I thought. And then a huge sort of tremor ran through me. After so long, so much fantasizing, I'd actually kissed him. I hope he didn't see that shiver, I thought. I don't want him to know how overwhelmed I am, not yet.

"Better go," I said, huskily—I hope it was huskily. I needed to get away before my knees buckled completely. "See you Saturday."

"See you," he said. And I managed to turn my bike around and we were off in opposite directions.

I'm not quite sure how I got home after that. But I did somehow.

"Coll, *please*," Val was groaning. "If you tell me *one* more time how *erotic* it was when he got hold of your stupid hair, I'm going to pass out!"

"OK, OK, OK," I said. "It's just that—"

"I mean, there's only so much I can take. I've been listening for the last *hour*."

She had, too. And she'd been absolutely delighted when I told her that It Had Happened. I'd been out to eat with Art, and we'd had the most amazing snog in the history of the world.

She'd got a bit odd when I told her we'd made a date to see Schroedinger, though.

"But Greg said he was going to try and get tickets for that," she said. "He's bound to have got one for you."

"Is he? Well, if he has he can easily land it on some-

**56**

one else. They're meant to be really good."

"Yes, but he'll expect you to go with him . . ."

"Well, too bad! I didn't say I was going with him. Come on, Val, this is my big chance!"

"Oh, I know that. It's just that he'll be really upset if he sees you there with hunk features. You know he will."

"Look, Val, Greg's not my boyfriend. What are you going on about?"

"I just know what he feels for you," she said darkly, and we left it at that.

As we were going home, I saw Sam and Tricia standing by the school gates, chatting together. When we walked by, they both stopped talking and turned to stare at me.

"What are you smirking at?" said Val.

"Oh, nothing," I answered.

# NO. 12

I didn't bother going down to the Center that Friday night. I also persuaded Val to tell Greg that I'd already got a ticket to see Schroedinger, and that I was going with someone else. It's not that I didn't want to face Greg exactly, but I wanted a night in on my own. I had all that thinking about Art to do.

I wanted to rerun last night through in my mind, for a start, every fabulous minute, with lots of slowed-down action replays. And then I wanted to kind of project ahead about Sidwells. I had to decide what I was going to wear. I'd set quite a precedent with my new swimsuit. I went through all the jeans and leggings and sweat-shirts I owned and rejected the lot. They were OK for normal everyday wear, but this wasn't normal everyday.

In despair, I mooched downstairs to make myself a cup of coffee. It was really quiet—Sarah was at one of her gruesome sleepovers, and Dad was late back. Mum was sitting in her usual place at the kitchen table, sur-rounded by work papers and empty mugs.

She looked up and we exchanged sort-of smiles. She

was wearing a new floppy scarf that she'd draped round her shoulders. It had rich, autumn colors, and it suited her. Butter her up, I thought, and maybe she'll give you an advance on your allowance.

"I like your shawl thing, Mum," I said, but she just shrugged and carried on flicking papers about.

As I selected a dirty mug from the collection on the table, Mum asked me to make a cup of coffee for her, too. Then she started asking me questions. She wouldn't be fobbed off, either—she knew something was up. She wanted to know why I hadn't gone out as usual that night. And why I was so late getting back the night before. And why I looked so happy for once.

In the end I told her. Not all the details—just that I'd met someone swimming, and I was going to meet him at Sidwells tomorrow night.

"I see," she said, tightening her lips a little. "And how does Gregory feel about this?"

"Mum, Greg has nothing to do with it! He isn't my boyfriend!" Maybe I should get that tattooed on my body somewhere.

"Well you could have fooled me. You were out with him only last week. Does HE know he isn't your boyfriend?"

"Does he? Yes! Of course he does! We're just friends who go out together sometimes!"

"I see. Just friends, eh?" And she smiled, eyebrows raised, in that infuriating way she has.

Then she probed a bit about "this-new-young-man" and I answered sulkily. She wasn't too hostile, though. I think the fact that I'd met Art swimming gave an air of purity to the relationship as far as she was concerned. She probably imagined some clean-cut, clean-living youth, sublimating all his sexual urges in healthy exercise, while I did the same. If only she knew.

"I wish I had something good to wear tomorrow, though," I wound up in a rather whiny voice. "I'm so sick of all my stuff."

"Oh, Colette, don't be so tedious. Nothing to wear, indeed."

"Well, I haven't. Nothing good."

"Well, why don't you go out and get yourself something tomorrow?" she asked. "If it's that important."

"No money," I answered.

"Honestly, Colette, I don't know where all your money goes."

On extremely expensive swimsuits, I thought.

"Why don't you look through that bag of stuff Auntie Gwen sent down?" she went on.

"Why don't I *what?*" I squawked.

"You heard," said Mum.

Auntie Gwen was Mum's older sister, and she'd sent down this bag of old clothes for me, in the fond belief that some of it was back in fashion. I'd taken one peep inside, seen a lot of purple and green polycotton, and shoved it in the cupboard under the stairs with all the other things nobody wanted.

"Some of that stuff was quite nice, Colette," Mum said reprovingly. "Biba. Quant. You might at least take a look."

So, more to shut her up than anything else, I did take a look. I dragged the bulging binbag from under the stairs and tipped it out on the kitchen table. And she was right, hiding in among the horrors there was some quite nice stuff: old, embroidered, made-in-India smocks; some aubergine velvet trousers that I knew I didn't have a hope of squeezing into; and this beautiful, beautiful shirt.

"Oh, wow!" I said, as I held it up against me. "This is *fabulous!*"

"You SEE?" crowed Mum in terrible triumph. "You SEE? That would be off the rails in five minutes in an Oxfam shop. It's absolutely LOVELY!"

And it was lovely. It was long and loose, made of heavy cream linen, and very simple, almost masculine in cut. It had just a trace of arty-looking embroidery on the back and sides in slightly darker cream. I peeled off my T-shirt there and then and pulled the shirt on. It smelled a bit musty, but it fitted. It felt great.

"Button up the sleeves," said Mum. "And wear it with your black jeans. That's all you need." I stared at her. She was right. Extraordinary as it seemed, Mum had taste!

I shot upstairs to look in my bedroom mirror. It was perfect. It looked different, special, but not weird enough to make me stand out. And it felt right. It felt like me—branching out a bit.

As I was pulling on my black jeans to make sure they'd go, I heard Mum stomp upstairs and go into her room. A few minutes later she appeared at my door, holding a tiny suede drawstring bag.

"Here," she said, tossing it to me. "Since you're into old things."

I loosened the string and tipped its contents into my hand. Three heavy silver rings fell out. One had a black stone set in art-deco coils. One was a huge tiger's eye on a thick band. The third was a woman's face disappearing into leaves and branches. All three were stunning.

I looked up at her. Was she giving them to me? What had come over her all of a sudden?

"I've hung on to those rings for longer than I care to remember," Mum said. "I saved up for weeks to buy that tiger's eye one. Do you like them? I'm sure I've seen ones a bit like them in the jewelers. Back in fashion."

"Mum, they're brilliant," I breathed.

"I always used to wear all three together," she said, pleased. "They look good all together. It just came to me that they would go perfectly with that shirt. Same age, for a start!"

"They fit," I said as I slipped them on. "They fit perfectly."

"Well, they're yours, then. I couldn't get them on now if I tried!"

**62**

In answer I threw myself at her and gave her a huge hug. It was like being enveloped by a big, soft sofa. She really could be OK. I felt a bit sad as I thought how rarely I hugged her nowadays.

Then she stood back and surveyed me. "You look really good," she said. "Talk about a time warp, though. Don't go adopting all those old views on free love to go with the shirt, will you?"

Mum went downstairs and I spent some time admiring my be-ringed hands, and how the shirt set off my dark hair. So this was what they'd worn when everyone was doing it all the time with everyone else, I thought. Then I peeled off the shirt to give it a careful wash by hand.

# NO. 13

**S**aturday night arrived, and I showered and put on my wonderful new-old shirt and the rings. I brushed out my hair and left it loose. I looked different, I felt different, and I was so excited I felt a bit sick. I deliberately left it quite late before I set out to walk to Sidwells. I aimed to get there about five past eight. I wasn't going to have a repeat of all that angst at the pool. Art could wait for me this time.

I suppose it was because I was nervous, but I felt pretty lonely walking by myself into the center of town. I'm so used to going places with Val, or with our group—Greg and Dave and Rachel and everyone. Maybe I'd got stuck in a bit of a rut with them, but it was safe in that rut. Now I felt as though I'd cut myself adrift. It felt like a big risk, setting out alone to meet this stranger. Where would I be if it all went wrong?

Oh, grow up, I told myself, and stepped out with a bit more vigor. But I wasn't all that confident he'd be there, even after the great time we'd had on Thursday night and the kiss and everything. An awful churning started in my guts. Suppose I got Stood Up? Not exactly a fun thought to dwell on.

When I got there, Sidwells was buzzing. People were meeting friends, going through the doors, self-assured, noisy, adult. I felt like a real lightweight, the only person on her own. I scanned the crowd anxiously. I couldn't see Art anywhere. *Again.*

This is torture, I thought, in sudden babyish panic. I can't bear it.

I made myself walk across the entrance to the pub, past a crowd of bikers. Still no sign. With a jolt of real panic I looked at my watch. It was nearly ten past eight. I've left it too late, I thought. He's given up on me. He's gone in on his own. If he ever came in the first place.

My anxious eyes gave one last despairing swivel. Strangers everywhere. Then, a bit further on, I saw someone leaning up against the wall, in a brown leather jacket . . .

Art.

"Coll!" he shouted, and in four strides was beside me. I worked hard to keep the joyful hysteria out of my smile.

"You're late," he said. "I thought I'd been stood up." But he didn't sound too stressed about it. He got hold of my arms, just above the elbows. "Give us a kiss, then," he said, with almost shocking self-confidence.

So I did.

I don't think it was instinctive for either of us to stop

kissing once we'd started, but something well-brought up inside me, that told me you simply didn't snog in front of public buildings when you've only just said hello, made me pull back fairly soon. But I felt great. It was happening with him, it really was.

"Come on, let's go in," he said. "I said I'd see some mates at the bar."

I felt a bit disappointed when he said that, but told myself it didn't matter. He gave the doorman two tickets and we walked into the hall. Once again I had that wonderful, hooked-up feeling, walking beside him. I'd forgotten all that will-he, won't-he anxiety. I was holding his hand and risking eyeball strain swiveling them sideways to look at him and I felt great.

By the bar, a short stocky bloke with a sneer for a smile and a horrible waistcoat was hailing him. "*Art!* Over here! Art and his new amoroso! She hasn't stood you up then? What a *tremendous* disappointment! I'm just waiting for the day you get ditched by a woman, you bastard! Hello, Colette—it is Colette, isn't it? I'm *Mark!*" And he swooped forward and planted a kiss on my cheek.

Short of having a neon sign saying *I'm a wanker* stapled to his forehead, Mark could not have made it more clear that that was what he was. I mumbled "hi" and looked up at Art, frowning.

"Mark said he'd give us a lift home," Art said, quickly. Then he jerked his head toward the two standing next

**66**

to Mark, saying, "This is Pete, and this is Sally."

They were all out of the same mold: public school twits. Pete was kind of pale and washed out, and Sally was puffy and venomous looking. I said hello. They both stared at me fixedly.

Mark asked Art and me what we wanted to drink. You could tell he had a phenomenally stacked wallet.

"When's the band supposed to start?" said Art.

No one answered him. I was glad he seemed keen to get away from his friends, though. I certainly was.

Mark turned back from the bar with our drinks. "Nice *rings*," said Sally, in a prissy voice, looking at my hand as I took my drink. "Unusual."

Whenever anyone says "unusual" like that, I always think they want to add "not many people would be seen dead in them."

"Thanks," I said. "They were my mum's."

"Your *mum*'s?" snorted Sally, in disbelief. Her mum obviously only wore diamonds. "Was she a hippie or something?"

"Yes," I said, coldly. "A hippie or something. She still is."

Art took hold of both my hands and looked down at my rings. "They're great knuckledusters, Coll," he said. "I like them."

"An armed woman, ay?" drawled Mark. "Better watch it, my son."

Art put his arm round me and buried his nose in my

hair. Pete sniggered and put his arm round Sally, who shrugged it off with a violent twitch of the shoulders. There was a long, icy pause.

Art's friends were obviously seriously fun people to be with.

Then, happily, there was an announcement. Schroedinger were about to start. We moved over to get in front of the little stage just as they started playing.

Their music was loud—good and bluesy, the sort I like. The bass made the floor beneath us vibrate. If I'd been with Val, I thought, we'd have been moving about by now. But from the look of Art's mates, dancing wasn't on the cards.

Anyway, I was holding hands with Art and I was sort of dancing inside. I could feel this creamy little smile spreading itself across my face.

Pull yourself together, I lectured myself. Stop acting so *smitten*. He'll think you're a complete moron.

So I started really concentrating on the music, moving my head to the beat. We swayed, and applauded, shouting the odd comment to each other over the noise. Then Art put his arm around me and as the music got louder, I slowly worked my way further under his arm and slid my arm around his back. It felt hard, warm. His leather jacket was around us like a cloak, a shield. I inhaled its smell, its grown-up, male smell. I moved my head against his chest and even risked a brief nuzzle of his neck. Careful, I said to myself, you'll pass out.

The interval came, and the band walked off the stage, sweaty and happy. They knew it had gone down really well. Art said he'd get more drinks. Pete went to help him, and Sally trooped off to the bog. I was left alone with Mark.

"So! Colette!" he said, like somebody's pompous great-uncle making conversation. "How long have you known our friend Art, hmm?"

"Not long."

"Bit of a smooth operator, our Art, eh?"

"How do you mean?"

He laughed—a loud, patronizing, men-only-club type of laugh that made me want to knee him. "How do I mean?" he said. "Well, you should know." And he did the horrible laugh again.

I looked over toward the bar, hoping Art was on his way back, and saw Val and Greg and a few others from our group standing there. Val was giggling at something Greg had said and they were both looking toward me. It had to happen, I suppose, meeting like this. I'd known they were going to be here.

I waved, and Val and Greg walked toward us, the others coming along behind. Val looked amused and aghast at the same time.

"Hi, Co—oll—" she said, slowly, as she rolled her eyes toward Mark.

Suddenly it dawned on me that she thought Mark was *him*. "Oh, you don't think this is . . ." I shrieked,

**69**

stopping myself before I got really insulting. "This is Mark," I said firmly. "He's a friend of Art's. Mark, this is Val, and Greg, and Rachel, Dave and Caro."

Mark homed in on Rachel right away. She's quite pretty, kind of delicate-looking, but shy.

"Hell . . . o!" he oiled. "How are you enjoying it so far, as they say?"

Rachel smiled nervously. I felt awful, subjecting her to such a creep. "It's good . . ." she whispered. "I think they're good."

"Oh, *good*," said Mark.

"Their new bass player's all right," said Greg, coming to her rescue. "He's brought the whole band together. They really pushed it out on that last number . . ."

Then he trailed off and his face changed, and I knew that Art had come up from behind to join us, and Greg had realized who he was. At first Greg looked a bit stunned—then wounded, somehow. In retreat. I felt a flash of guilt. Greg's not my boyfriend, I said to myself.

I turned round. "*This* is Art," I announced. "Art, this is Val—and this is Greg . . . and Rachel . . . Dave and Caro."

"Hi," said Art, his voice even deeper than normal, as he handed me my drink. "What d'you think of the band?"

"They're great," said Val, staring at him. She had that look she gets when she's sizing someone up. "I'm really enjoying it."

There was a pause. Greg was looking down at the floor. I was torn between pity for him and massive, ego-ranting pride. I wanted to kind of freeze frame everyone so I could say to Val: Well, was I right or was I *right?* Isn't he a *babe?* But that would have to wait.

Pete and Sally joined us, and I introduced everyone again, and then we all stood round in an awkward bunch. There was a sort of chilliness around us, a waiting.

"Greg said the bass player's new," I babbled, trying to keep things going.

"Yeah, he is—joined them about two months ago. He's the one I got the tickets from," said Art, as if that was just ordinary stuff.

"How do you know him?" asked Dave, impressed despite himself.

"Oh, he used to do music sessions for my old man. He's backed a couple of ads. I'm glad he's doing something real at last," Art said, and he smiled. He really does look gorgeous when he smiles. And then he put his arm around me.

The chill around the group intensified.

"Cigarette, anyone?" asked Mark, waving a packet under our noses. "Art? Oh no, you don't, do you? It might make you short of breath. Might interfere with your performance . . . on the field, of course." Then he gave that horrible laugh again.

It was the final death knell to any more socializing. In our group, hardly anyone smokes, and we're pretty down on that sort of sexy innuendo crap—in fact, up to now it's been me who's been loudest in its condemnation. Art just ignored him, but I began to feel I'd gone over to the enemy camp. Greg looked as though he'd shut down completely, and Val was looking critical.

"Well, they're going to start again soon," she said, taking Greg's arm. "Let's go and find our places."

"Great to meet you," said Pete, and we all sort of smiled and said "bye" and walked off.

"Are they *good* friends of yours?" asked Sally, snidely.

"Very good," I said. I felt I owed them that at least.

# NO. 14

**I** felt a bit upset as I walked back to the stage. But then Schroedinger got going, really loud, and soon I forgot all about Greg and Val and Sally and Mark. The band finished up with some slow numbers and Art put his arms around me. We were too close to dance properly, and I was so happy it hurt. We didn't kiss—well, it was all a bit public. Every now and then I'd glance over Art's shoulder and see Sally watching us.

Then the band said goodnight and thank you, and we clapped and hollered and stamped, and they came back for an encore, another fast one, and we all danced about to it. Then it really was all over, and everyone was moving outside into the darkness and the cool clean air. Mark unlocked his car, and Art pulled open the back door and got in, still holding on to my hand so that I practically fell in after him. We were both laughing.

"*I'll* sit in front, shall I?" said Sally in an acid voice. Pete clambered into the back, and we were off. I was in the darkness next to Art, feeling his creaky-leather-covered arm around me, and his face very close. Too soon, Mark screeched to a halt outside my house.

I thanked Mark for the lift but couldn't bring myself to tell him how nice it was to have met him. I opened the door and climbed out, and Art followed me. Mark bellowed after us, "You've got *three* minutes, Art. That long enough for you?"

*Cringe.*

"Is he a *close* friend of yours?" I asked, as we stopped in the shadow of the big holly tree by our front wall.

"No. Feel free to slag him off."

"I will—what an idiot! Does he always act like some fifty-year-old businessman in a strip club? It's so . . . embarrassing."

"Forget about him."

"What a *jerk* though. How do you *stand* him?"

Art laughed. "I'm used to him. Now shut up." And he put his arms around me, and we started kissing. Pretty soon one of his hands was sliding round to the front of my shirt. I didn't exactly mind, but I was greatly inhibited by the fact that if Mum chose that moment to look out of her bedroom window, she'd see everything.

I wriggled away. Art seemed to take that in his stride. "Look, I can't get out during the week at the moment. Things at home are—not good. I screwed up some exams, and the old man went crazy. He just about lets me out Thursday nights to go swimming."

"Poor you," I said, holding my breath.

74

"Give me your phone number, anyway. We could meet Thursday."

As I was scribbling my number on a bit of paper Art found in his pocket, Mark sounded the car horn loudly.

"*Blimey,*" I squawked. "Look, *please* don't bring him along next time. I'd sooner walk."

"You're on." He grabbed me for one last lovely kiss, and ran back to the car, shouting "I'll phone" over his shoulder.

I felt like I might combust as I let myself in the front door. I felt like a riot, like a circus. I danced silently up the stairs, lay on my bed and relived every moment of the evening. I was so gone on Art now that it scared me. Dancing with him, kissing him, holding his hand . . . I closed my eyes and floated and dipped and dived in that wonderful, obsessive, frightening feeling for a while.

Then a little doubt set in around the edges, and that scared me, too. It was to do with Mark, and those snidey comments he'd made, about Art being a smooth operator and so on. What was Art doing, having someone like Mark for a friend, anyway? Didn't he have any *taste?* No one needs lifts that badly. And Sally—what was going on there?

Then I moved on to think about my friends, and how awful it had been when we'd all tried to talk together. It was Greg I was thinking of as I fell asleep. I remembered his face when he saw Art come up to join me and he realized that we were together. I hoped he wasn't feeling too bad. I hoped he'd find someone soon who really wanted to be with him, like I wanted to be with Art. Everyone deserved that. Whatever came of it.

On Sunday morning I lasted until 10 o'clock and then phoned Val. "Can I come round?"

"Yes," she said. She didn't need to ask why.

Twenty minutes later, she opened the door to me. She seemed a little cool as we made our way through all the heaps of dogs and kids upstairs to her bedroom. Her house is a mess, too, just like mine, but her Mum—unlike mine—really works hard trying to stop it being one. It's just that the dogs and kids always defeat her.

I shut Val's bedroom door behind us, flopped down on her lumpy old bed, and said, *"Well?"*

"Well *what?*" she said, thrusting her chin out. Then she burst out laughing. "Oh, OK! Look at you—your eyes are manic! OK, you didn't exaggerate! He is an absolute babe!"

"Isn't he? Isn't he? I *told* you he was. I can't *believe* I'm going out with him."

"Neither can I. He's *way* out of your league."

"Oh, don't. Don't say that."

"Come on, I was joking. Sort of. So what's he like? Does he snog as good as he looks?"

I frowned with disapproval at the crudity of her words. Then I said, "He snogs like an angel."

"OK, OK," sniggered Val, "I admit it, I'm deeply jealous."

I laughed, delighted. Then I sat there and made Val feed me—delicious stuff about how sexy he was, how deep his voice was, how altogether desirable he was. How great his hair was, how long his legs were, how beautiful his face was. I even made her enthuse over his leather jacket. And then the conversation took a downer. She started to talk about his friends.

"Honestly, Coll, I thought they were losers. That Mark character he was with was a real creep. What does Art see in him?"

"A lift home, I think," I said.

"Oh. That figures. And what about that female— Sally, was it? She looked at you as though she hated you. Is she one of Art's exes, or something?"

"I've no idea," I answered, loftily.

"We still live in a sexist world," she sighed. "Why did you have to join his lot? Why couldn't you have brought *him* over to join *us?*"

"Well, maybe I will, next time," I said.

"Only don't bring his mates with him. I really didn't think much of his mates, Coll."

"Look, I think I've *grasped* that," I said, a bit needled. "And I'm not going *out* with his friends. It's *him* I'm interested in."

"They're real public school types, aren't they?" she

went on. "Which school does Art go to?"

And I had to admit to her that he went to the Loughborough, a newish private school with a reputation for first-rate facilities and fantastic fees.

"But that's his dad's choice," I added. "He didn't want to go there."

"Maybe not. But it figures, him going there. He did look pretty flashy."

"Flashy? What d'you mean, flashy?" I was getting really pissed off with her now.

"Well, he had that sort of sheen about him. Spoiled, you know."

"Spoiled?" I spat. "What d'you mean *spoiled?* You mean he gets too much sweets money? Five Action Men for Christmas?"

"No," she replied, in an irritatingly reasonable voice. "But he looks as though he's used to getting what he wants. He looks *bloody* sure of himself. That's all."

I was silent. I couldn't argue with her on that point.

"You're trying to tell me I don't stand a chance with him, aren't you?" I said, sulkily, after a pause.

"No I'm *not.* I'm just saying—I'm just saying be careful. You sound so smitten. When you talk about him you sound like your brain's gone missing, and I just don't want you to get hurt. That's all."

I smiled at her. "Look, Val, I can look after myself. If it doesn't work, it doesn't work—I can cope."

She smiled back. She must have known it was all

bravado. Then she said, a bit carefully, "Greg was pretty upset last night."

I groaned. "I thought he looked upset. But I am *not* his girlfriend!"

"I know, I know you're not his girlfriend, and he knows it, too, but he really likes you, and he kept on hoping it would work out between you. He must have felt absolutely wiped out when he saw Art; out of the contest. I mean, take them on the outside, and there is no contest, is there?"

But on the inside? I thought, and out loud I said, "What did he say to you?" Was it concern or vanity making me ask?

"Not much," she answered. "But he was really down. I felt really sorry for him."

"I should call him," I said.

"I wouldn't," she said quickly. "I'd leave it. When are you seeing the Boy Wonder again, anyway?"

"He's phoning me," I answered.

# NO. 15

He's phoning me. What torture lies in that innocent little phrase. *When* is he phoning me? I didn't have his number. I had to metaphorically sit by the phone, like some passive female from the 1950s, and wait.

Monday evening was all right. I was still high from Saturday, and I thought it was probably too soon for him to call anyway. Besides, I wasn't going to be waiting around by the phone, because Monday night was self-defense night.

As soon as I got in from school, Mum told me firmly that supper would be early, so that I wouldn't be late for my class. She knows that I try and wriggle out of going sometimes. And she brings all her energy to bear to stop me.

I ate the meal silently, then reluctantly went upstairs and changed into my combat gear. As I got my bike out and wheeled it down the path, Mum stood by the door and watched me, smiling. The way she saw it,

I was continuing my training to be a fully fledged foot-soldier in the battle of the sexes.

The self-defense classes are run by one of Mum's man-hating friends, Sonia. Sonia is very fit and very fierce. It is pure joy to her to think of Threatening Men being thrown through the air and against walls by Women Who Have Trained. If you Have Trained, it is a positive boon, apparently, to be Threatened. In fact one week I expect her to lose her rag completely and shout "Get in first, girls, don't wait until they attack you! They're going to one day—they're men! When you see a man on his own, *paste* him! Do it for your sisters!"

Sometimes I quite enjoy the self-defense classes, though. For all her manic zeal, old Sonia is a good teacher, and knowing a bit about self-defense makes me feel more confident when I'm out and about. But this Monday, defending myself wasn't exactly uppermost in my mind.

I wandered through the sports center doors, a moony little smile on my face as I remembered coming through them with Art, last Thursday. That seemed so long ago now. So much had happened since.

I trooped up to the exercise room. Sonia was standing by the door, checking everyone off. She has short spiky bleached hair, and a sharp little face—wiry and mean, like a terrier. She looked like once she'd got her teeth into a Threatening Man she wouldn't let go until he was good and bloodied.

"OK, everyone!" she called. "We all seem to be here. Let's start."

And we were off. All the basic moves, again and again, drilled into us so that we'd have them at our fingertips if we were ever attacked. Sonia moved among us, making criticisms and suggestions, then she called a halt.

"OK, that's fine. Now for the second half, we're going to look at something a bit different. We're going to look at Date Rape."

Oh, *please*. I felt this little hysterical giggle form deep inside me, gather speed up my windpipe and try to force its way out of my mouth.

"There's nothing funny or trivial about Date Rape," Sonia went on, looking hard at me, "and it's getting more and more common. You're out with someone you're attracted to, someone you're beginning to have a sexual involvement with. He gets too pushy. You're confused. You're not sure at what point to call a halt. That's the danger. You're not in charge, and you're not clear in your mind that there's a real threat. You still think you can handle it with words and body language; you don't want to hurt this guy's feelings."

She paused. The look on her face said that, far from worrying about hurting his feelings at this stage, she'd be setting about hurting his skull with a heavy ashtray.

"That's the danger," she went on. "Not recognizing that you've passed the stage where normal communication will work. You've got onto the next stage—when you need to defend yourself. That's what we're going to look at now."

"She's getting more psychological every week," I muttered to my neighbor.

"I know," my neighbor replied. "I think she's wonderful."

And we moved onto role play: the snog that turns nasty; the snuggle that gets out of control. I couldn't help it, I felt sillier and sillier. When Mave pinioned me against the floor and I was supposed to jerk my knee up and roll sideways, I had this overwhelming longing to fling my arms wide and shout "Take me! Take me!" I didn't do that, but I did laugh. I just couldn't treat it seriously. I couldn't believe that anyone I went out with was going to push things farther than I wanted to go. Not Art. Not anyone. Why did Sonia have to put us through all this negative stuff?

I hated the way women were made to feel frightened the whole time. And I hated the way all these warnings made sex seem so threatening—as though it had nothing to do with liking, with caring. It was pretty depressing to be learning how to defend myself from the bad side of sex when I hadn't exactly got into the good side yet.

Sometimes it felt like I was surrounded by a conspiracy to put me off men for life.

# NO. 16

Tuesday night was dominated by the hope that Art might phone. I did my homework; I watched telly; I paced about my room. The phone did ring twice, but both times it was for Mum. It was awful. I felt really stupid for caring so much. Not until it was 10:30 did I relax a bit. He'll phone tomorrow, I told myself, the day before we'd said we'd meet.

Wednesday night was even worse, of course. If he didn't phone then, I'd had it. I felt wretched. I couldn't bear the silence from the stupid machine. Then it finally rang at about eight, and I shot down to answer it.

"Hello, is that Colette? Could I speak to Justine please?" It was Claire, sounding tearful. I was so disappointed I didn't say a word, just thrust the receiver at Mum. The phone would be tied up for hours now. I couldn't bear it.

"Mum, I'm going for a walk," I hissed at her, as she sat shaking her head in outrage at whatever was coming down the phone into her ear. She ignored me.

I stamped out of the house and walked and walked,

up into town and back again. I kept repeating to myself that of course he liked me and of course we'd see each other again. It had been a good idea to get out of the house. It meant I was spared the torture of the silent phone. And when I returned, a message would be waiting for me, like a present. Wouldn't it?

It was well after nine by the time I got home. I could hear the telly from the back room. I walked toward it, muttering "please, please, please."

I put my head around the door.

"Any messages?" I asked, in a strangled voice.

There was an unbearable pause, then Mum said, "Oh yes, yes—a young man called. Ark, was it? It wasn't Gregory, anyway. He wants you to phone him back."

My heart leaped, then it plummeted. "I haven't got his *number!*" I wailed.

"He gave me it." Mum looked at me sternly. "It's by the phone."

I raced to the phone, seized the paper, kissed it, and with trembling fingers punched out the number. As I heard it ring, I felt a fresh wave of panic. I was going to be speaking to him soon, and I didn't know what to say. All this panic and suffering, wave on wave of it. Why does being smitten have to be so exhausting?

Finally, after seven rings, a young, silvery voice answered. I felt a kind of cold horror until I realized it must be the stepmother.

"Hi, hello, may I speak to Art, please? It's Colette here."

"Sorry, who did you say you were?" the silvery voice replied. Not a great start.

"Colette."

"Hang on, I'll get him."

I sat there, heart pounding, strangling the receiver in my sweaty grip, imagining him coming down the stairs, coming out of a room somewhere . . . And then I heard his wonderful deep voice.

"Hi, Coll. How's it going?"

"Hi, hello, Art—fine, it's fine. How are you? Look, I hope this isn't too late to phone . . . I'm sorry I wasn't in . . . I went for a walk, quite a long walk . . . and Mum's been on the phone most of the night—she's had about five calls or something, well, that's what it feels like . . . have you been trying to get through?" The thinking part of my brain heard this drivel in horror, but it seemed to have forgotten where the off-switch for my mouth was.

Luckily, Art interrupted my ravings. "No, I got through. Look, what about tomorrow? Can you make it?"

"Make it? Yes, sure," I said, a bit shrilly.

"What d'you want to do? Shall we meet at the pool? We could swim, and then go into town—or we could give swimming a miss and just find a bar somewhere."

A bar. How sophisticated. He didn't mean a Wimpy bar, I was sure of that.

"I don't mind," I said. "What do you think?" I can be dead decisive sometimes.

"Well, why don't we swim first, then go on somewhere.

That way I'll still come home smelling of chlorine, and I'll get my allowance next month."

I laughed. "Sure. What time?"

"Can you make it by seven? Then we'll have more time afterward."

"Seven's fine."

"See you in the pool, then."

"Great. See you tomorrow, then. Fine. Seven. Great. Goodbye, then." And as he said goodbye my brain managed to direct my hand to hang up before I could witter on anymore.

I sprang up the stairs. On the landing, I collided with Sarah. I picked her up, hugged her very hard, and set her on her feet again.

"Muuu . . . uum!" she wailed.

Then I shot into my room and snapped on my radio— it was playing some grim old schmaltzy tune but I loved it, I adored it, I sang along to it. I danced about the floor in triumph, jumped on the bed, jumped off again. "He wants more time afterward," I sang to myself. "He wants more *time*." And a big gloating smile spread itself across my face.

# NO. 17

This Thursday I felt almost confident. No worries that Art wouldn't turn up. I'd got to the pool and was standing by the lifeguard's high chair when I saw him walk out of the changing room. He came up to me and put his arms round me, and we kissed. I could feel the lifeguard's disapproval shooting down like an electric current. They don't like that kind of thing at the pool. So we dived in, had a chaste swim, and then got dressed and made our way into town.

We cycled round some winding back streets to a small wine bar and locked up our bikes in the alley beside it. I must have looked a bit intimidated as we went through the door because Art said, "It's OK, I've got some money." He walked with confidence up to the bar.

I was worried that we wouldn't look old enough, but the man behind the bar actually seemed to recognize Art. He bought a couple of bottles of beer, ordered some food, and we made our way to a table.

Half-term was coming up; we talked about it in low voices so no one would hear us and know that we were still at school. I told Art that, as usual, I had absolutely no plans for it whatsoever. It was just great to be off the grindstone for a week. Then Art announced he was going to France for most of it. I felt like I'd been punched, but I managed to smile in an interested sort of way.

"Fran's idea," he said. "Friends of Dad's have a big house near Paris, and they're always on at us to go over. Dad's hardly been home for the last few weeks—tied up at work, well, that's what he says—and last night Fran threw a fit and said they had to get away or she'd leave him." He smiled; he seemed to enjoy the idea.

"Do you have to go with them?" I asked, hopefully, as the waiter slammed our food down on the table.

"Yeah, I do," he said, between mouthfuls. "I don't want to—but Dad won't let me stay behind on my own. Not for a whole week. Doesn't trust me." He paused, grinning. "Not after last time."

"When will you be back?" I asked, casually. I hoped it was casually.

"The end of next week. The old man won't survive being separated from his stupid company any longer than that. He's only agreed to go at all because there's a fax in the house. Look, we're not going till Sunday. Why don't you come over Saturday? We could go out—we could take the bikes out somewhere."

The invitation was like a reprieve. I could see his house, find out about him, fill in all the gaps. We ordered some coffee, and I relaxed into the smoky atmosphere of the place, and we talked. I wished we could have held hands across the table, like the couple just across from us, but I didn't have the nerve to make the first move.

After a while I looked at my watch and saw it was after ten, and said I had to go. We walked out to the alleyway alongside the bar, where we'd shackled our bikes. Art put his arm around me, and as soon as we'd got around the corner away from the glare of the street light he turned to face me, and we started necking. It was wonderful, touching him, tasting him, breathing him in, after all that time just looking at each other across the table. I didn't close my eyes right away—I wanted to see him, know him. Then after a while I did close my eyes. Art was so good to kiss. It felt as though all of him was behind it.

He pulled back and said, "You really know how to do this, don't you?" Then something seemed to shift, and he wrapped himself around me, and we were into a really frenzied session, like nothing I'd experienced before. At first it was great, it felt—I don't know, as though I really turned him on—but after a while it got a bit too much. I could feel how strong he was. I'm strong, too, but I thought maybe he'd be the one to win in an arm wrestling contest. And then he started undoing the buttons on my shirt, and I felt myself being maneuvered backward, against the wall, and suddenly all that stuff about date rape flashed into my mind. Shut up, Sonia, I

**90**

said to myself. You know nothing. I'm fine.

I'll do a test, I decided, to see if he's still reading my body language, my "that's far enough" signs. I turned my face away and pulled away a bit.

He failed the test. He didn't read my body language, he just got hold of me again. Or maybe he *did* read my body language. To be honest, I wasn't sure what was going on with my body anymore.

"You don't smell of chlorine, like you wanted," I said, trying to bring some words into play. "You smell of beer."

"That's OK. You smell fabulous," he said, and moved in again.

This time I pushed him backward and said, "Let's go." He made a noise a bit like a groan, a bit like swearing, and moved away. We unlocked our bikes and rode off in silence. When we reached my turning, Art told me his address, and said he'd make lunch for us on Saturday before we went out. Then we parted with a subdued kiss, a goodnight kiss.

Curled up in my bed that night, I went into a marathon brooding session. Why do blokes have to *do* that, try it on anywhere and wait for you to call a halt? It was nerve-racking. It was like enjoying a nice ride and suddenly finding the acceleration zooming up to 120 mph.

And why did guys have this thing about speed? Can't they enjoy taking it slowly? Get to know you first?

Art and I didn't know each other, not yet. I had no real idea what he was thinking and feeling, or what he thought of me. I felt all this incredible energy between us, but maybe it was all my energy, reflecting off him, bouncing back to me. I could be just another girl in a long line for him. He needn't be keen on me at all. He could be just keen on sex. How was I supposed to know?

I rolled over onto my back and stared at the ceiling. You *can't* know, yet, I said to myself. You'll just have to see how it goes. Stop analyzing everything to death. It's happening. What you most wanted to happen is happening.

Then I went to sleep.

# NO. 18

"Look at you," said Val as we met at the school gates on Friday morning. "The cat that got the cream—*bathed* in the cream. No need to enjoy it all quite so much, Coll. Think of the rest of us and our pleasureless existences."

"What—*what?*" I said. "I haven't said a thing. And you can't use 'pleasureless' like that."

"Just did. And you don't need to *say* anything. Come on, how far did you get on the Petting Chart?"

"Oh, grow up, Val," I said. "We went to a *wine* bar." I didn't see the need to mention the alley. It sounded a bit sordid.

"Just checking," she grinned. "What about tonight? You seeing him tonight?"

"No, Saturday. I'm going to his house."

"See how the other half live, ay? Well, come out with us tonight then. I think everyone's going to the Dog and Duck. We missed you last week."

"Yeah, OK. Well . . . maybe."

"Oh, for heaven's sake—don't put yourself out too much, will you?" she said, and walked off.

When the evening came round, though, I gave the Dog and Duck a miss. I don't know, I just didn't feel like going out. Mind you, if I'd known there was going to be a meeting of the Wailing Sisterhood in our kitchen that night, maybe I would have gone out after all.

About four of them turned up, one after the other, all clutching little offerings to leave at the feet of the great white goddess, my mother: wine, shortbread, olives, no flowers.

I shot upstairs to hide in my room when I heard the first one arrive, but by 9:30 my craving for caffeine got so strong I had to risk a foray into the kitchen.

"Hello, Colette," one of them said as I came around the door, and they all sort of bleated at me in chorus:

"Not out, tonight, Colette?"

"Not seeing that nice young man—Greg, wasn't it?"

"Better than a lot of them, he was. I thought, anyway."

"Urgh, boys. You're better off without them, Coll."

Mum's snort silenced them all like a command. "We haven't seen Gregory around recently. Colette seems to have found herself a new-young-man."

She said it like that, new-young-man, as though it was all one word, a species of lowlife slug or something. I hated it.

The chorus started up again.

"Well, be careful, darling! You can't be too careful!"

"Young men—hormones on legs. I remember . . ."

"They *can* be such animals, can't they? I say that, and I've got a son, but . . ."

"Goodness, Justine, you say you haven't met him? Aren't you worried? I remember when my daughter . . ." and so on and so on.

I turned my back on them and made coffee, then I shot upstairs as fast as I could without spilling it. When I got to the landing I pulled down the old wooden sliding steps to the loft, climbed up, and pulled the steps up after me.

Bliss. I was alone among the junk and cobwebs, and I couldn't hear the Sisterhood anymore, not even a distant murmur. I sat down under the grimy skylight and drank my coffee. I go up to the attic when I really want to be on my own. It's wonderfully far away from everyone. A whole story's worth.

The attic would make a fabulous bedroom. For years I've battled with Mum to let me have it. It's a proper room, built with the house, and it's large. Its big skylight window is aimed straight at the clouds. It has a wooden floor, and a sloping ceiling on two sides. You can stand upright in a lot of it. There's an old oak railing round most of the hatch in the center of the room, to stop you falling through when the hatch is open. The railing divides the room up, and makes it feel really special.

But Mum won't hear of me taking it over. I've given up asking. She says my grim little box is a perfectly good room. She says the loft's useful for storage. She says sleeping up there would be a fire risk, because I could get cut off and fry. She says it isn't heated properly, and I could freeze. She says no.

I stayed sitting on an old packing case for what seemed like hours, and then I went down to bed.

# NO. 19

I rode round to Art's house the next day, feeling extremely nervous. Time to see the creature in his natural habitat. Time to flesh out the few terse facts he'd told me about his home. Time to meet his dad and stepmum.

I freewheeled up to what I thought was Art's place and checked the number. My jaw dropped. Wow, this *was* it, then! I'd prepared myself to be impressed, but this was a mansion. Long drive, big gates, tubs of greenery—the whole place reeked of money and style. I left my bike round the side and knocked tentatively.

Luckily, it was Art who opened the door to me. He looked fantastic, as usual. And he looked at home.

"Hi!" he said. "Come in."

I stepped into the hall and stared around me at the beautiful rugs, the gleaming furniture, and the just-this-side-of-daring pictures on the wall. Wealth, possessions—they shouldn't change the way you think about someone, but they do. You start to see them through this veneer of privilege. I felt a bit shaken as I followed

Art through the hall. What must it be like to live like this? What did it do to you?

As we passed an open door, a man's voice called out, "Art! Aren't you going to introduce us?"

I watched Art's shoulders tense up, and then collapse again, resigned. "Oh, come on," he said, going through the doorway. A man stood as we entered and came smilingly toward me. You could see the family resemblance immediately. He had Art's handsome straight nose and his green-gold eyes. He was tall, like Art, with lots of gray hair and tanned skin. He must have been about fifty, but he was still good-looking. I suppose I must be attracted to that gene type.

"Well!" he said. "So this is . . . ?"

"Colette," said Art, without expression.

"Colette! Delighted to meet you! I'm Ian." He took my hand and pressed it, briefly, with lots of deliberate eye contact. "Art's dad—but I expect you've worked that one out for yourself."

I squirmed, and smiled goofily.

"This is Fran," he said, waving an arm toward a woman still seated on the sofa, "my wife."

Fran was a lot younger than Art's dad, and she looked fabulous. She looked as though she was waiting for some magazine to come and interview her. It was midday on Saturday, slobbing around time, and yet she was all made up, hair sleek, wearing casual, costly clothes on her thin, stylish body. She looked silvery, like her voice had sounded on the phone. I felt like a clod-hopping girl guide in comparison.

She held out a graceful hand toward me, her left hand, and I wondered in panic if I was supposed to kiss it or something. But she just waved it a little and said, "Hi, Colette!" The way she pronounced it, *Hi* had about five syllables. It took her about ten minutes just to get it out of her mouth.

Then she looked at Art. "This is your healthy friend, is it, darling? Who you met at the pool?"

The *healthy* friend? Was there an unhealthy one, too, then? Some decadent bitch who drank and shot up and smoked fifty a day?

Art just ignored her. "Well, let's get some lunch, so we can get going," he said.

As we walked out of the room Fran's voice followed us. "Art, darling, don't completely wreck the fridge, OK?"

"What does Fran stand for?" I whispered to Art.

"Frankenstein," he replied, without a hint of a smile.

We went into the kitchen, and once again I had to deal with the turbulent emotions of envy, admiration, disapproval, desire. The kitchen was breathtaking: balanced, beautiful, huge. You could have fed the entire population of China for a week on what it must have cost. And you could have seated a fair proportion of them around the massive central cooking island while you were doing it.

"What an amazing room," I said, and Art shrugged.

"Does Fran work?" I asked. I was still whispering. Let's face it, I was in awe.

"Oh, she does a few things. She used to work on a magazine—fashion or something. That's where she met Dad—ad campaign. Now she just does stuff for friends, people who can't fire her. Interior decoration, that kind of crap. Anything to do with how things look, that's Fran."

"It must take up a lot of her time, this place," I said.

Art laughed. "Yes. Their lifestyle takes up all her time." He started scooping bread rolls out of a big bin. "Find some ham or something in the fridge, will you?" he said. I found the ham and within a couple of minutes we were perched at one end of the huge cooking island, eating. I looked at him as his white teeth bit into the bread, and forgot about being impressed by my surroundings.

"I thought we could make it out to Coddleston," he said. "It's about ten miles—not far. There's this timewarp of a tea shop there."

"Not *far?*" I squawked. "Ten miles? And back again? You believe in pushing it, don't you?"

"What's the matter? You're fit enough. You know you are. We can work up an appetite. It does great cream teas."

Then Fran came through the door. "Oh good, you've found something," she said, looking at our crumbs with disapproval. "I'm going to make our lunch. Colette, darling, d'you want some salad with that?"

I smiled, said no thank you, and she started pulling stuff out of the fridge—limes and fresh herbs and olives and big tomatoes, not the sort of food normal people have for lunch. Then Ian walked in. "Want a hand, my love?" he asked.

Standing by the long, wooden counter, chopping up salad together, they looked like an advert. I gawped shamelessly. Here was a scene of "man sharing domestic work," just the way Mum says it should be, but I knew instinctively that she wouldn't approve. She'd hate it. They were enjoying it too much.

Fran said something to Ian and he laughed and put his arm around her shoulders. They were murmuring to each other, mouths about one inch apart. And then his hand slipped down her back caressingly. And then *her* hand slithered sort of strokingly around his waist. I couldn't have been more gobsmacked if a troop of Chippendales had burst into the room and begun hip-thrusting toward me. This was sexual activity—between parents!

I sat fiddling with my coffee mug, trying to look as though I was used to this kind of stuff. Art swallowed the last of his roll indifferently, stood up, and said, "Want to see my room?"

I nodded and followed him out of the kitchen, up the wide staircase and into his bedroom. I felt a bit twitchy when he shut the door behind us, but I didn't show it. I looked around me, and said, "Nice."

It wasn't, though. It was weird. The decor was as plush and elegant as the rest of the house, and all Art's stuff looked completely out of place. You kind of expected a maid to walk in and dump all his junk in a binbag and put the room back to normal.

I picked my way past piles of jeans and sweatshirts on the floor. "Ever heard of coathangers . . ." I began, turning back toward him. He was so close behind me we practically rubbed noses.

"Don't believe in them," he said, putting his arms around me. "And you haven't said hello to me properly yet." Then he kissed me, nuzzling at me, trying to turn it into a real clinch.

"Art," I said anxiously, into his mouth, "your dad is downstairs."

"He won't care," he answered. "They leave me alone." Then he half-lifted me, and we did this kind of ungainly backward shuffle and fell on the bed together.

Somewhere deep in my mind warning sirens were wailing. But when he kissed me again, I kissed him back.

"They won't come in, Coll," he murmured. "They never do. Relax."

Relax. Oh, sure. Half a dozen things seemed to be going on at once. You're far too good at this, I thought. Too much bloody practice. I pulled away from him, and we practically wrestled across the bed until I slid off the

**102**

edge with most of the duvet and landed on the floor.

"*Shit!*" I said.

Art stood up. I couldn't see what his face was doing. He'd just better not be laughing, that's all.

He stood over me and held out his hand. "You OK?" he said. After a second's pause I let him help me up, but I couldn't look at him.

"Look, I've got the message," he went on. "If you don't want to get heavy yet, that's fine. Let's go."

It wasn't exactly an apology—in fact it was pretty arrogant—but I have to admit something inside me felt pleased. There was some kind of commitment in that "yet." It meant we had time.

As coolly as I could I followed him out of the room.

# NO. 20

Once we got out of town and on to the country roads, we both cycled really fast. It turned into a bit of a race. And I kept up with Art. I was determined to. It was about three o'clock when we pulled into Coddleston's little market square. We were both smiling with a sense of shared achievement as we locked the bikes up.

"Cuppa tea?" said Art, putting his arm around me.

The tea shop was all copper kettles and Toby jugs and white lace. An ancient waitress showed us to a table, and briskly made off with our order.

Art leaned toward me, grinning. "That was a terrific ride," he said. "I've never been out with a girl who liked biking before. Certainly not at that pace."

"You're not *that* fast," I retorted. "I had no trouble keeping up."

"Just as well I was navigating, though. You're a lousy map reader."

"And *you're* a boy scout."

He laughed and trapped one of my legs between his under the table.

The cream tea arrived. We wolfed down the scones, fighting over the last smears of jam and clotted cream. Then we sat back to drink the thick, pot-brewed tea. And I wanted to talk.

"Your dad's not how I expected," I said. "He seems really relaxed. I thought he'd be some kind of ogre, keeping you in to work."

Art looked at me, a bit cynically. "His power's in his wallet," he said. "If I mess up, I end up poor."

"Art, is your mother . . . ?"

"She's dead."

"Oh . . . I'm sorry." There was a silence. "When . . . ?"

"Five years ago. I was twelve. It was cancer. It was quick."

"It must have been awful."

"It was. Dad went mad. Lots and lots of women around, trying to blot it out. And then Fran came along, and nailed him."

As he said this, he signaled abruptly to the waitress, and we paid the bill and left. I wondered if I'd been clumsy, crass, asking about his mother, but in a way I didn't care. I wanted to find out about him, all of him.

We set off back for home, slower this time, side by side when the road allowed it. The sun had grown thinner, and I felt cold as I pedaled. As we grew nearer to

**105**

town this sad, dreading sort of feeling came over me, because I knew he was going to France, and we wouldn't see each other for a whole week.

We reached his house, and got off our bikes and stood there, a bit indecisively. "Do you want to come in?" he asked.

"I'd better not," I said. "You've got to pack and everything, haven't you. I'd better go." I wanted to get the goodbyes over with. I felt this big lump growing in my throat.

We moved toward each other and hugged. "I'll see you when I get back. I'll phone you. Maybe Friday, if we can drag Fran away by then."

"That would be great." Friday—it seemed like years away. "OK, then, bye. Send me a postcard."

We had a long, long kiss, and another, then I set off home.

# No. 21

When I got home I felt a bit like I'd been on one of those weird sci-fi trips. You know the sort of thing—when you travel in a time-loop. You return to Earth after masses of adventures and feel like years and years have gone by and you're different, you've changed completely. Then you discover you've got back only minutes after you'd originally left. Nothing's changed, and no one's missed you.

That was how I felt, walking through the front door. Ever since I'd met Art, I'd been on this trip. And now he'd gone again and I was back. It was Saturday night, the start of half-term, and I had nothing to do. I felt this great empty vacuum closing round me.

I wandered through to the kitchen. Sarah was cutting out trolls' clothes on the table; Mum was slashing into a cauliflower over a load of saucepans in the sink; and the cat was nestled into a pile of dirty washing on the floor.

"Hi, Mum," I said. "Hi, Sarah." They ignored me.

Yes, I was back.

○ ○ ○

I went to bed early that night, and woke up late Sunday morning. I felt like I was on hold. The four times I'd been out with Art hung in my mind, obsessing me. I searched for details that proved he was as smitten with me as I was with him. I worried about what he might be doing in France. It took up all of my time. I could have phoned Val, I suppose, and seen what everyone was up to, but I somehow didn't want to. I felt so out of touch.

By Monday I was beginning to feel a bit guilty about not contacting Val, but I really didn't want company. Instead, I shut myself up in the attic, and thought. About Art, and how everything had moved on some-how. And about sex. About the fact that I was a virgin and Art almost certainly wasn't, and what I was going to do about it.

Sex—it's a different country, isn't it? I mean, if you haven't been there, you don't know what it's like, no matter how much research you've done. And there's such a weird attitude to it everywhere. Even though it's chucked at you from all sides—to sell ice cream, to get rid of politicians—no one really talks about it properly. Not about what it really is.

We had a sex education lesson once in year eight. It was completely embarrassing. Our games mistress, beet-root red, waved some grim looking diagrams around as she went through the facts. Then she jumbled up a few vague words like "morality" and "caring" to put the whole thing in a human context, and asked for questions. Hardly anyone asked any because we all just wanted to get away and stop watching her suffer.

Anyway, I already knew everything she was talking about because Mum believes in telling kids the Facts of Life from an early age. I honestly can't remember when I didn't know how babies are made. Mum encouraged us to discuss abortion and AIDS and everything round the dinner table. It's enough to put you off your food sometimes.

And that's the trouble. Mum's great on diseases and problems, but not so good on pleasure. Mum telling you about sex was like a music-hater telling you how an orchestra worked.

Trying to find out about sex on your own wasn't much better. You've got dreary textbooks telling you how to do it on the one hand, and swoony romantic novels telling you what to aim for on the other. I just couldn't see how the one translated itself into the other.

The first time a boy put his tongue in my mouth, I thought it was pretty disgusting. Now it's great. Suppose sex was like that? Suppose I found it awful to start off with?

And I had to admit that I was a real virgin. I mean, I'd barely even petted—not "below the waist" as Sam would nauseatingly put it. It always seemed like the stage before sex, and I'd never been with anyone I wanted to sleep with before. Until Art.

Now, when we kissed, when we held each other, I felt it could be him, it really could be. But I was still pretty scared by the whole idea.

That thing Art said in his bedroom, "We don't have to get heavy yet." It felt like half promise, half threat. What did "yet" mean to him? Two more dates? Two more months? The thing is, I wanted to know him, trust him a bit more first. I wanted sex to be part of the whole experience of getting to know him. I didn't want it sidelined.

And my inexperience weighed on me, like an inadequacy.

That evening, Val phoned me. We were both a little stiff with each other. She wanted to know why I hadn't come to the Dog and Duck on Friday, and I told her I just hadn't felt like it. She made some comment about the pub probably not having much attraction after what I'd been up to on Thursday night. I told her about our bike ride, and seeing Art's house, and what a great day it had been. But there was a distance between us, somehow—she was pleased for me, but not that pleased, and I found myself playing down most of it, not going into details. Or feelings.

Then I told her that Art had gone to France for most of half-term, and she said "oh" in a really knowing and irritating way. It annoyed me so much that when she said—in that case, why didn't I come out tonight with everyone? They were going to hang out for a while and maybe go for a pizza—I said no. I regretted it almost as soon as I said it, but I didn't feel I could go back on it. I told her I had stuff to do, then I said good-bye and hung up before she could ask what stuff.

And I went back to my solitary thinking.

# NO. 22

**T**he next morning, disaster threatened. Mum had taken half-term week off to Be With Her Children, and by Tuesday she was bored stiff. So she suddenly got it into her head that we would visit Aunt Gwen. She had to be kidding. Quite apart from the fact that a visit to Aunt Gwen wasn't exactly a carnival, I wanted to be here on Friday when Art got back.

"Frank, what do you think?" Mum boomed as Dad came round the door. "A few days at Gwennie's—get the girls some fresh sea air—it would be a nice change for all of us."

"We're-going-to-the-seaside!" sang Sarah.

"Mum, I really don't want to go," I said.

"You were only saying last night you didn't have much work on at the moment," she carried on to Dad, ignoring me. "Claire can feed the cat. If I phone Gwen now we can set off first thing tomorrow."

"I can't, Justine," said Dad. "I've got a meeting on Friday afternoon up in town."

"Well, can't you rearrange it?" she asked, annoyed.

Mum was always annoyed when anyone's plans interfered with hers.

"Hardly. It's been set up for weeks."

Mum snorted.

"And Colette just said she didn't want to go," Dad continued. "So she could stay here with me."

Mum turned to look at me, eyebrows raised. "DON'T you want to go? You love it there!"

"Mum, that was when I was ten years old. I'd sooner stay here. I'll keep an eye on Dad."

So it was settled, almost painlessly. Mum phoned Gwen and started packing for an early start the next day. Disaster had been averted.

That night I heard Mum and Dad arguing in their room. Maybe she was trying to make Dad change his mind about going to Gwen's. I hoped not, because Mum usually won their arguments, and if he went, I'd have to go along, too.

Next morning I awoke to the smell of frying bacon, and Dad standing over my bed with a cup of tea. He was smiling.

"Come on," he said. "Get up and have some eggs and bacon and wave Mum and Sarah off to the seaside. Oh, and put some old clothes on. You and I have work to do."

"Work?" I said sleepily. "What work? It's my half-term, Dad!"

But he'd gone. I pulled on some old jeans and a T-shirt and arrived in the kitchen just in time to stop Sarah giving my share of bacon to the cat. Mum was heaving suitcases into her car, and rapping out instructions to Dad about getting shopping in, and Sarah kept whining on about me taking care of her hamster. Then they were off, and a wonderful calm settled on the house.

"OK, Dad," I said unenthusiastically, "what's this work you want me to do? Are you going to clear up the garden or something?"

"No." He looked at me, poker-faced. "We're clearing out the attic."

I felt dizzy with hope. "Clearing out the . . . ?"

"Attic. For you."

"Oh, Dad! You're joking! You're going to let me . . . ?"

He nodded, grinning.

"That's just *fantastic!*" I squawked. "But—but does Mum know?"

"Yes. We talked about it last night. She's not keen, as you know. But I said it was ridiculous to waste all that space when you'd make such good use of it."

My attic, I was going to have my attic. I couldn't believe it. I could hardly speak. "Let's get started!" I said.

# NO. 23

I felt ecstatic as I pulled the ladder down and climbed up. It was like being given a huge, beautiful present out of the blue. Dad followed, full of enthusiasm and commands.

"First of all," he said, "we have to sort all this junk out. Now, there's two big cupboards at the back there, under the eaves. The stuff we really can't throw away we can store in those."

We set to. We crammed the cupboards to bursting point with the camping equipment and Christmas decorations, and we hurled all the old clothes and ancient lampshades and piles of newspapers down through the hatch onto a big sheet that Dad had spread below. For two hours we hauled and heaved, until at last the attic was empty. It looked bigger than ever. All that glorious space echoed around us, and it was mine.

"Right," Dad said. "You make coffee; I'll see if I can get this window to open."

I shot down the ladder. Dad was great when he was like this—positive and full of energy. When I climbed up again with two mugs he was fiddling with a screwdriver at the side of the skylight.

"Nearly there," he said. "Just a bit rusted over. It's completely watertight—they knew how to make things in those days. Look at this brass handle, it's lovely. Pass me that oil can—yes—here we go." And he slowly rotated the huge window round, through 180 degrees, so that the moss-covered outside was on the inside.

"Over to you," he said. "Clean up the window—let some light in. Then start washing down the walls. I'm off to the dump. Then I'll buy some paint, and pick up fish and chips on the way back for lunch. Right?"

"Right!" I said, saluting. I was hopping about with excitement. Never had cleaning held such allure. Well, any allure, actually. But this was different.

"White paint?" said Dad.

I looked at the stained, grimy walls. "White paint," I said.

When Dad had gone, I took a scraper and my radio up to the attic and got to work. I felt so happy, here on my own cleaning the window. It was almost as if I was moving into my own flat or something. And I realized I'd hardly thought about Art all morning, which was quite a relief. But it all felt connected, somehow. It was still about me changing, branching out. I couldn't really explain it.

When I'd got the outside as clean as I could, I

swiveled the window around like I'd seen Dad do, and cleaned all the dust and webs off the inside. Then I stood back to admire the effect.

High spring sunshine slanted through the glass, shining on the floor. The window was gleaming, and all the dazzling light it let in showed the room to be absolutely filthy.

But I was on a roll. I rejoiced in all the grime. I fetched a long-handled broom, turned the music up, and danced and lunged about, sweeping all the webs and dust from the walls and ceiling. Then I swept the floor and started washing down the ceiling and walls. I kept staggering down the attic steps with filthy water and staggering up again with clean. Just as I was washing down the last wall Dad shouted, with excellent timing: "I'm back, Coll—come and get it!"

I finished cleaning the last corner and dashed into the kitchen. Dad was unwrapping the fish and chips. My stomach contracted with greed and hunger.

"Blimey," I said, in surprise. "I'm starving!"

"I bet you are," he said. "It's two-thirty and we've been at it since nine."

We ate in friendly silence, and then, as we sat over big mugs of tea, and the food hit my stomach and redirected most of my energy to my digestive system, I realized how tired I was. My arms ached from wiping down the walls, and my legs ached from charging up and down the ladder.

Dad was still raring to go, though. "Right! Let's see if we can get the first coat on, woodwork and walls. Then we can slap another coat on tomorrow and move you in by nighttime."

"You mean I can sleep up there tomorrow night?" I asked, delighted.

"If we get cracking I don't see why not."

"Dad, I'm going to phone Val. She likes painting. Maybe she'll come and help—is that OK with you?"

"Sure it is," said Dad. He liked Val.

Val was at home. I half felt I should make some sort of apology or explanation to her, but I thought that could come later. I told her about moving into the attic, and she sounded really pleased for me. She even sounded pleased when I asked her to come and join in the painting. She said she'd be over right away.

"You *lucky* thing," she breathed, when she'd climbed up the ladder. "All this *space!* It's going to be fantastic!"

Dad was at work, rubbing down the woodwork. He chucked a packet of sandpaper at us both, and said, "Start rubbing down over there, and we'll meet in the middle. Rub with the grain, remember."

"You should have come out with us last night," said Val as we worked. "We never seem to see you nowadays."

"Oh, I know," I said in a low voice. "Look, I'm sorry I was so snotty on the phone. I just feel . . . weird at the

**118**

moment, you know?" I couldn't really go into details with Dad just across the way, but Val nodded as though she understood.

"In the end, only Greg and I went on to get a pizza," she said. "We *just* had enough money. We had a great time, though. He really is a good bloke, Coll."

"I know, I know!"

"What about Friday? Coming out with us then?"

I thought about Art maybe arriving back on Friday. "Maybe," I said. "Maybe I will."

The rubbing down was finished. We cleaned up, scrubbed the floor, and then Val and I stood back and watched in sheer pleasure as Dad applied the first stroke of the roller to the walls. The broad, gleaming white stripe seemed to cut through all the dingy gray. It shone, reflecting light from the window.

"This is going to be stunning when it's finished!" exclaimed Val.

"Don't stand there gawping!" Dad said. "Get a little brush each and fill in the edges for me!"

So we crouched, and we painted, and Dad followed us with the roller, and within an hour the whole place had had its first coat.

"I'll make some tea," I said. The light was going. Dad flicked on an uncovered bulb hanging in the center of the attic and a dreary yellow light filled the place.

"Spots," said Dad. "You need spotlights, and lamps.

There's lots of power points up here. I had it rewired when we did the whole house."

I started to climb down the ladder to get the tea. "Bring some biscuits up with you!" Val shouted down after me.

Over tea the three of us admired the room, congratulating each other for working so hard. Then we set to and undercoated the woodwork, and when that was finished Dad went down to have a long soak in the bath. Val and I sat under the skylight, planning my attic, where to put the spotlights, what kind of rug to get.

After a while, she said, "So when is Art meant to be coming back, then?"

"Friday," I said. And suddenly I felt really lonely—not so much for him, for her. I'd missed her; I'd missed telling her everything, feeling that we were both in it together.

"Oh, Val," I said, "I'm sorry I've been a cow. I don't want to cut myself off from everyone, it's just that—well—I can't seem to think of anyone but him at the moment. I think he might be the one, you know?"

Val stared ahead. She knew what I meant. Not the one forever, maybe, but the one for now. The one to cross into the other country with.

"You always were so black and white," she said. "So—extreme. I wasn't mad at you, for not coming out and everything. It's just that I think it's a bad idea to drop your friends just 'cos you've gone and got smitten with someone. Not just for our sakes—for yours."

I put my arm around her shoulders and hugged her. "There's no way I'm dropping you. You're a good mate, you know."

"The best," she retorted, grinning. "Now come on, spill it. What's he *really* like?"

So I told her.

## NO. 24

**D**ad set the alarm for eight the next day, and we got stuck straight in and finished off the painting. Lunchtime saw us down on our hands and knees, rubbing wax into the floorboards. Then we grabbed a sandwich, shifted up the furniture from my old room, and set off for IKEA. Dad said he had to keep going—once he stopped, he wouldn't move for the next month.

Soon I'd chosen spotlights, a bright Aztec-looking rug, two lamps, two huge floor cushions, and a window blind. As the trolley mounded up with purchases I protested—"Dad! This is so *much!* Should we get this all at once?"

"Coll, it's all cheap and cheerful and, more to the point"—he wheeled the trolley purposefully toward the check-out counter—"I am not making a return trip to this place if I can help it."

Three hours later, the spotlights and blind had been installed, and the rug and cushions were on the floor.

The place was transformed. It looked absolutely great.

"Over to you now, Coll," breathed Dad, as he finished adjusting the spotlights. "I personally am not coming up that ladder for the next year."

I went over and hugged him. He'd worked so hard for me—I felt choked up to think back on it. "Dad," I said. "Thank you. It really is wonderful—I can't tell you."

"I know," he said, putting out a hand to ruffle my hair. Then he climbed a bit stiffly through the hatch and disappeared.

I pulled up the ladder after him. Then I curled up on the new floor cushions, hugging myself with happiness. I gazed all around me and felt really lucky to have a Dad like mine. I thought about Val and felt so glad to have her as a friend, glad we'd got back together again. Then I rolled over onto my front and thought about Art and I was filled with this incredible yearning. I saw his face close up; remembered his taste, his smell, his neck where his hair touched. It seemed ages since I'd last seen him.

Dad and I had a scratch dinner that night—we were both too exhausted to cook. Then he disappeared into his office and I slumped in front of the telly for a while. At about nine o'clock, Dad came into the back room, waving a sheet of paper.

"This fax has just emerged from my machine," he said. "It's for you. Not content with monopolizing the telephone, it seems the young are taking over all other forms of communication, too. A *fax,* for heaven's sake. Whatever's happened to romance?"

My heart somersaulted. I seized the sheet of paper and scanned it. In scrawled capital letters it said:

THIS IS INSTEAD OF A POSTCARD.
NOT AS PRETTY, BUT A LOT FASTER.

I AM BORED OUT OF MY MIND HERE.

I'LL BE BACK FRIDAY.
THAT'S TOMORROW.

MISS YOU. ART

That night I slept blissfully up in the loft, with the fax next to me. I woke early on Friday morning, swung my legs out of bed and took great pleasure in letting up my new blind and seeing all the light sweep in. Then I pulled on a tracksuit and went out for a run. He's coming back today, he's coming back today, I said to myself over and over, in rhythm with my steps. He missed me, he missed me. Even knowing Mum and Sarah were returning on Saturday couldn't spoil things. I jogged for maybe half an hour, then headed home.

Turning into my street, I slowed down. A car had swerved rather wildly to a stop a few meters ahead of me. Greg's mum's Astra. Greg sprang out and ran toward me, shouting, "Coll! Coll, hi!"

It was so good to see his familiar, humorous face again. I threw myself at him and gave him a huge hug.

"Where have you *been?*" he said, laughing, as he hugged me back. "I haven't seen you for weeks. Just 'cos you're going out with some poser who wears black leather, there's no need to go all isolationist and ditch your old friends."

"I *haven't!* And it's brown leather. He wears brown leather."

"Whatever. Good job you never really made it as a veggie, anyway, or you'd be faced with a moral crisis every time he put his arm around you. I mean, leather! Uggh!"

I hugged him again. He was handling the arrival of Art with humor, and I loved him for it. "What are you up to now?" I asked. "Come in for coffee? It's safe. Mum's not around."

"OK," he said. "But you've forgotten—I *like* your mother."

"Nobody likes my mother—not even a pervert like you. Come on, I've got something to show you. You will *freak.*"

I made us toast and coffee, and headed straight up the attic steps. At the top, I turned to watch Greg's face.

He didn't disappoint me. "Wow! How did you pull this one off? You did some deal with your Mum? You drugged her? Killed her?"

"No! She's been away for the past two days. It was all Dad's doing."

After he'd admired everything about the place, we sat down on the big floor cushions and ate the toast and talked. He told me he'd seen quite a bit of Val, and they'd both missed me. As we talked, the shadow of Art hung between us like some kind of sexy specter, and after fifteen minutes or so, he made it into the conversation.

"So," said Greg, "this new bloke—he's got it, has he? The X factor? What it takes?" His eyes had hazed over a bit as he said that, and you could tell he'd made up his mind to be mature about the whole thing. I wanted to go over and hug him again, but I stopped myself. "He's certainly got looks," he went on ruefully. "I hated him on sight."

I laughed. "I think he's a bit of a sleaze—you know, lurid past. And Val thinks he's spoiled. The whole thing is probably doomed." Did I really think that? I remembered the wonderful fax again. What was I—superstitious, now?

"Well, he's got taste, anyway," said Greg. "He's gone for you."

I smiled. "I haven't seen that much of him. He's away this week."

"But when you are with him, it's mind-bogglingly good? Go on, tell me. I can take it."

"Oh, Greg. Stop being an idiot. You're a friend. You'll always be my friend." Greg bowed, a bit sarcastically. "Yes, it's good," I went on. "I'm really keen on him—and I think he likes me. But he's a bit, well, it's a bit tense, sometimes."

"He's an animal, isn't he? I knew it."

I laughed. "He is a bit pushy. I mean—we don't really know each other yet, but he seems to . . . I don't know where I stand with him, not really."

"I don't believe I'm hearing this. Colette Rowlands—never afraid to lay down the law about men—what's happened to her?"

"Oh, shut up. All that was theory. It's very different when you're . . ."

Greg looked down at the rug. "Look, Coll, this may be out of order, but Val told me you were getting all messed up about him. She thinks you ought to relax about the whole thing. Just tell him to back off. Blokes like that are . . ." And he stopped. I wanted him to go on, to give his opinion, as a male and everything, but I didn't say anything. It would have been pretty crass to discuss my sex life with Greg.

I shrugged, and said, "It'll work out—if it's meant to."

Then we moved on to safer ground, and just chatted. It was so easy, being with Greg. He made me laugh; I felt relaxed with him. Art, well, that was not relaxing. There was too much energy between us. It was like a magnet, and it was like a wall.

Greg made me promise to go to the pub with them all that night. He also said that this girl we knew, Linda, was having a party on Saturday. He said to bring Art along so he could hate him all over again at close quarters.

"And if Wonderboy comes on too strong at the party," Greg added, "just let Val know. She'll sort him out."

I laughed. Well, at the time I thought he was joking.

# NO. 26

I spent the rest of the day mooning about, hoping for a call from Art. By 7 P.M. I still hadn't heard anything. I'd also completely lost patience with myself. "He's probably not even back yet," I told myself firmly. "And you are behaving like some kind of lovesick twerp. Now phone his house, and if he's not there, leave a message, and then go out and meet everyone." As soon as I'd told myself that I felt a bit sick, because it was so much the right thing to do that I knew I'd have to do it.

I dialed Art's number, and got Fran's silvery voice on the answer machine. I slammed the receiver down before the message ended. What was I going to say? I rehearsed a few things in my mind, then I made myself dial again.

The message came again, the beepbeepbeep went. I took a shaky breath. "Hi, Art, it's Coll. Thanks for your—" then I stopped, because I didn't think Art would have asked before he sent the fax, and it must cost a fortune to send faxes all the way from France "—*message*.

I'm out tonight, but there's a party tomorrow and maybe—I thought maybe you'd like to go? Anyway, give me a call—Bye!"

I replaced the receiver, hunched up on the chair and let out a muffled howl. Inside my head I played back my message. "I sounded like a complete *prat!*" I wailed to myself. "I hate those things! I sounded like a complete inarticulate *prat!*"

Then I made myself go and get ready to go out. After a while I began to feel better. After all, I'd taken charge. I was going out to meet my friends, and Art could phone me tomorrow.

I'd like to say that I had a great time that night. I'd like to say that it was good seeing all my old friends, and we had a good laugh. But it wasn't, and we didn't. I think everyone else enjoyed themselves, but I felt as though the plug had been pulled on me. I felt mechanical, not really there. I made myself make an effort, but no amount of determined cheerfulness could change things. It was as though Val and Greg and Rachel had been suspended, somehow. They were in the background. All my energy was focused on Art. It was scary.

Mum and Sarah arrived back early the next morning, and a great hubbub followed as everyone trooped upstairs to inspect the attic.

Mum criticized the choice of rug and thought I could

131

have managed with two spotlights instead of four, but I could see she was impressed despite herself. "It looks so big!" she kept saying, "So bright! It puts the rest of the house to shame!"

Sarah was bouncing on my bed, looking mean with jealousy. "What about *my* room?" she squeaked. "Can we redecorate *that?*"

Dad started talking about redoing the living room and Mum was talking about turning my old room into an office for her, and then, through all the din, I heard the phone ring.

I shot downstairs to answer it.

"Coll. Hi, it's me."

A great sigh started up in me at the sound of his voice. But I had to try and act normal.

"Hi! How was France?"

"Like I said—boring. How was your night last night?"

I smiled, triumphantly. He'd sounded almost put out.

"Oh, OK. Not brilliant," I said, as though I was so used to clubs and parties I got a bit fed up with them. "What about this party tonight? Can you come?"

"Sure," he said. "Great. Where?"

As coolly as I could I told him the address and said I'd see him there about nine.

Then I only had about ten hours to get through before I was with him again. Compared to all the hours in last week, that'd be a cinch. I filled it partly with deciding what to wear to the party, and partly with wanting to see Art so much that I felt I could hardly breathe.

I spent nearly an hour in the bathroom that evening, getting ready to go out. I heard Mum stomping past the locked door a few times, and phrases like "She's STILL in there" and "Goodness KNOWS what's come over her" floated through to me.

When I got to the party, Val and Greg were already there. "Well?" Val demanded. "Have you asked him?"

"He's coming," I said.

We went into the kitchen to get drinks, and stood around chatting and pulling lumps of French bread apart. I was too preoccupied to eat any, though. Every nerve in me was taut.

Suddenly Linda burst into the kitchen. "There's this gorgeous gatecrasher at the door!" she announced. "This woman just dropped him off. She looked dead glam. He must be her toyboy. Anyway, I've let him in."

I pushed past her, and made my way slowly, super-stitiously, to the front door.

"Colette?" I heard someone say. "Colette Rowlands? Yes, she's here."

And there he was, in the doorway, smiling. I felt that charge, that shock, of wanting.

He walked straight over and put his arms around me. "Thanks for your *fax*," I said, with a bit of sarcastic stress on the "fax." "I missed you, too."

"So give us a kiss," he said.

"Well," I could hear in the background. "Coll can obviously vouch for him."

"Yes," said Linda. "Damn."

The party really got going. Lots more people arrived, the music got turned up, and I had a brilliant time, laughing, dancing, introducing Art around. Val was quite nice to him, although I got the feeling she was waiting for him to suddenly try and rip my shirt off or something. Greg made a real effort to be friendly, too. The four of us had quite a long conversation together in the kitchen. It was dominated by Greg being funny—he was on form, although he also seemed a bit nervous to me, wound up. Still, he made all of us, including Art, fall about laughing. Maybe Art *can* fit in with my friends, I thought.

Toward midnight, when people began to slow down and couples began drifting off to corners, Art said, "Come on. Let's find somewhere quiet for a while."

"What about here?" I said, flopping onto the end of a big settee someone had just vacated. He joined me, a bit slowly.

**135**

"You haven't told me about France," I said.

"Nothing to tell."

"But what's the place like—where you stayed?"

"Big. Boring. Coll, I don't want to *talk!*"

I laughed, and we started necking, making up for all that lost time. It was like Art was trying to work out who I was by touch. Through half-closed eyes, I saw the couple at the other end of the sofa get up and walk rather primly away.

"Art," I said, somewhere into his chest, "Art. Let's get another drink." I pulled on the hair at the back of his head. "I need a drink," I said.

Slowly, he stood up, and followed me.

We rummaged about in the mess in the deserted kitchen; I found an unopened bottle of soda water and Art filled a plastic glass with lukewarm beer from the bottom of a barrel. Then we leaned against the sink, looking at all the wreckage. "It's been trashed," I said. "There must be loads more people here than they invited."

"Gatecrashers," he said. "Like me. I heard that girl call me a gatecrasher."

"Did you hear what else she called you?" I said, laughing. "Anyway, you're not a gatecrasher. You're legit. You're here with me."

"Yes," he said. "I am." Then he drained his glass, took the soda bottle from me, and started kissing me again. I reached up and dug my hands into his hair, pulling his head down to mine. We wound ourselves around each other, tighter and tighter; after a while I felt him lift me up onto the counter behind.

"Art," I muttered. "What are you—"

"It's OK," he said. "It's OK."

Now our faces were on the same level. Somewhere on the edge of my consciousness I heard the door bang open once, but I kept my eyes shut, and whoever it was must have left.

Then a crowd of lads trooped noisily into the kitchen and started making these pathetic whoooer noises. It was like being hit by cold water. I slid off the counter and turned my back on them.

"Let's get out of here," Art muttered.

We headed for the stairs. "This is only the fifth time we've been out together," I reminded him under my breath. Or was I reminding myself? We went into the bedroom where we'd left our coats, closed the door, and kissed for a while against it.

"Come on, let's lie down," he said.

I didn't move.

"Come on, I just want to lie with you for a minute. I'm not going to get heavy—someone could come in at any time."

So we did. We lay very close and he just stroked my hair, slowly, slowly, and stroked my back, and then I kissed him. Maybe he meant what he'd said, I thought, that it was up to me how far we went . . .

I had no time to find out, though, because suddenly the bedroom door burst open, and Val burst in. "Oh, *sorry!*" she said, in histrionic surprise. "I just have to get to my coat, I need something from it."

Art pulled away from me and stood up. He looked angrily at Val, who was rummaging among the coats with enormous innocence, and then he walked out of the room.

"Look," hissed Val the minute he'd gone. "He's had a lot to drink. I walked in on you in the kitchen, Coll, you were practically doing it in the sink! I just thought—we thought—you could do with a breather."

I laughed, but I couldn't meet her eye as I slid off the bed. I wasn't annoyed with her, though, just touched by how protective she'd been. "I was OK, Val, honestly. He was OK," I muttered.

"Oh, God, I'm sorry!" said Val. "Where's he gone? He's walked out on you!"

"Look, it's OK, Val," I said again, "but I think I'll go after him."

# NO. 28

I looked through the main rooms downstairs, but I couldn't see Art anywhere. He hadn't really gone, had he? I was beginning to feel really worried, checking the kitchen for the second time, when I saw him. He was outside, leaning up against the wall by the back door, arms folded. I went out there. "Hey," I said. "Art."

He turned the same bad-tempered face on me that he'd turned on Val. "Where's your minder?" he said.

"What's up with you?"

"I don't like being policed, that's what's up with me. You told her to come up and rescue you, didn't you? What did you say—give us five minutes and then burst in?"

The resentment in his voice shook me. We'd only ever been pleasant to each other before.

"Oh, grow up, Art," I said. "Of course I didn't."

"Why did she suddenly appear like that, then?"

"She needed something—"

"Oh, come *off* it. Don't try and tell me that was coincidence."

"OK, she didn't need anything. She was looking out for me. She thought you were drunk. She thought—she thought I might want a way out."

"She thought *what?* What have you said to her? I told you I wouldn't push you into anything, didn't I?"

"Yes, you did say that," I answered. "But you don't always act it."

"What's that supposed to mean?"

"I mean you—I mean it's always so . . . why does it have to be so . . . I mean I sometimes feel it's just heading straight to having sex, that's all." My God, I'd said it. I'd actually said it.

"Well, isn't it?" he replied, with equal honesty. "In the end?"

"In the end, maybe. With you, it's there right at the *beginning.* Like in the first five *minutes.*"

He smiled at that, despite himself, and looked straight at me. I felt triumphant, as if I'd scored a point. And then I couldn't resist it. I had to put the boot in. "Ever heard that women like to take their time?" I said.

That did it. Never criticize a guy's technique—it's on page one of the *Cosmo* Rule Book. Art folded his arms again, and looked down at the ground. You're sulking, I thought. You're even a bit hurt. It made me feel quite tender toward him. Fed by the exhilaration I felt because of what I'd been able to say to him, I stood as close to him as his folded arms would let me, put my hand up to the back of his neck, and stroked it. "Come on, Art," I said. "It's not a big deal." He stayed motion-less. So I got hold of his arms and unfolded them. He played dead; he let them drop down like weights by his sides, but I could tell he was trying not to smile. I pressed up against his chest, then I pulled his head down and started kissing him.

He didn't push me away, but he was still very pas-sive. It felt really weird at first, and then it felt good. For once, I was setting the pace. And he wasn't that good an actor. I knew he was enjoying it.

"I like this, you not moving for once," I said into his neck. "I like you playing dead."

His mouth came to life. "Maybe you'd like to tie me up. You kinky cow."

"Come on," I laughed. "Stop sulking."

"I'm not sulking," he said. "I'm taking my time. Like you said."

At that my nails kind of spontaneously dug into his chest, and he yelped and jerked backward. Then he laughed, too, and that broke the spell. He put his arms around my neck and started kissing me back.

When we finally went back into the house, we realized that the party was over. It was after two o'clock, and people were leaving. Mum would have a fit if I rolled home much later.

I looked around for Val and Greg to say goodbye, and finally found them sitting on the floor together in a

141

corner of the main room. They didn't see me, because they were too wrapped up in each other.

Kissing.

"Go and interrupt," said Art, as he came and stood beside me. "Go on, tell her you think she's sitting on your coat and you want something from it."

I turned away. "Leave it," I said.

# NO. 29

In the cab home, despite Art's body leaning close against me, I couldn't stop seeing Greg and Val in my mind, kissing. My two best friends, together. Leaving me out. That's what I felt—left out. It was like being back at primary school again.

Oh, grow up, I told myself. Good for them. They'd probably just had too much to drink.

"Hey," Art was saying, "*Hey!* Do you want to come, or what?"

"Come? Where?"

"To the cinema. Tomorrow. With me."

"Sure. What d'you want to see?"

"Well . . ."

"Because I'm not sitting through some gory load of macho crap, if that's what you're into . . ."

We were still happily criticizing each other's choice of films when the cab drew up outside my house. My front door was wide open. Standing in the doorway was a huge black shape.

"Oh, no," I said. "Mum."

Art craned around me to look and gave a low whistle. "Sheeeez. She's *enormous*. What's she there for?"

"It's 'cos we're late. It's after two."

"Want me to come and apologize?" he said, reluctantly.

"No, it's OK. I couldn't do that to you. Oh, God. Look, see you tomorrow!" I clambered out of the cab.

"So THERE you are!" Mum boomed, as I ran up the path. "Is everything all right? I was getting VERY WORRIED!"

"I'm fine, Mum. It's fine, honestly."

She glared at the retreating cab. "At least he saw you home, this new-young-man. But it's two-fifteen in the morning, Colette. What about our agreement that you PHONE if it's much after midnight?"

"Oh, look, I'm sorry I worried you. I didn't realize how late it'd got."

"Obviously. Another fifteen minutes, and I was going to phone Val's parents. Or Gregory's."

I groaned. Thank heavens I'd pre-empted that. Not that Val or Greg would be home, anyway. They were probably still snogging at the party.

As I went up the stairs she called after me, "Colette, I hope you're being sensible. Don't go letting things . . . run on too fast."

Suddenly I felt incredibly tired. "I won't, Mum," I answered. "Night."

o   o   o

It was restful, seeing a film together. We compromised on a political thriller with lots of action. Art ate his way through an enormous bucket of popcorn and got really excited by the fights and car chases, although he pretended he hadn't. There was only one cringe-making sex scene to sit through, during which I could feel my hand getting embarrassingly sweaty in his; and when we walked home afterward we had an enjoyable argument about what had actually happened in the plot.

"Look," Art said, as we came to a halt outside my house. "Fran wants you to come to dinner on Friday."

"*Fran* does?"

"They're having this sort of dinner party on Friday. I've got to be there, and Fran told me to ask you."

Not the most gracious of invites, but I was really chuffed. "Well, yeah. I mean, I'd love to."

"Look, I'm not doing you any favors here. It'll be phony and boring. But," he went on, giving me a great smile, "it'll be better if you're there."

"I'll come," I said.

# NO. 30

It wasn't nearly as bad going back to school the next day as I thought it would be. Generally, I felt good about things. I had my attic room. Things were really moving on with Art. And I was looking forward to the dinner party on Friday—in a nervous sort of way.

The coldness that had been there between Val and me at the start of half-term had vanished, too. We had a good laugh about her busting in on Art and me at the party.

"Honestly, Val, I was touched," I said. "I didn't know you cared so much about my purity. With friends like you, I have a good chance of staying a virgin forever."

She got a bit round eyed. "It's got to that stage, then?"

"No," I answered. "No, not yet. Pretty pathetic showing on the Petting Chart still. Give us time."

"I like him," she said suddenly. "He was OK on Saturday. He's not such a jerk as I first thought—well, not quite, anyway."

Somehow, neither of us got round to saying anything about her and Greg kissing. Maybe it wasn't really important.

On Tuesday, I went out shopping after school with Val and bought a shortish dark-red dress to wear to the dinner, despite Art telling me just to wear jeans. When I met him on Thursday at the pool, I tried to plug him about who else would be there, but my questions seemed to cause him actual physical pain, so I stopped.

At last Friday arrived, and the end-of-week netball session was enlivened by being able to let it slip to Sam and co that tonight I had a big dinner party to go to at my boyfriend's house, with some advertising mates of his old man's.

Their extreme anguish on hearing this was pure pleasure to me. "Boyfriend" was a stab to their souls—but "advertising people" just about finished them off.

Val was egging me on, enjoying herself hugely. "What time's the car picking you up?" she asked with all the relish of a sadist twisting the rope on her victim's neck.

"Car?" croaked Tricia.

"Mmm . . . Well—the car's only for the way home," I said. "You know what they're like, these people, they always hire cars."

"That new dress you got is terrific," enthused Val.

"Well—I just hope it's good enough. Fran's so chic,

you know. She used to be fashion editor on . . . oh, which magazine was it?"

"*Vogue*, wasn't it?" said Val brightly. Beside me, I heard Samantha gave a little anguished moan.

"Anyway, don't worry," Val went on heartlessly, "that dress is just the sort of thing Art'll go for." She had absolutely no idea what Art would go for, but so what? We were after blood.

"Anyway, the food's bound to be fantastic," I added grinning, "And Art said there'll be *buckets* of champagne . . ."

"Oh, I *adore* champagne," gushed Val, who had maybe had it once at someone's wedding. "It's an aphrodisiac, did you know? So don't drink *too* much, OK?"

"I don't need aphrodisiacs," I said. "Not with Art. He's so gorgeous."

"He practically *is* an aphrodisiac." Val was pitiless. "What a babe. He'll see you home, won't he, in the car?" Then she delivered her final bodyblow. "Wonder what it's like snogging in the back of a limo?"

There was a general hate-filled sigh. Sam's gang had grown kind of pale and watery, as if grief and envy were slowly dissolving them. It was at this point we felt we had to stop and leave them to chew over the details. There's only so much pain you can inflict on others without beginning to feel a little sickened yourself.

# NO. 31

As soon as I got home from school that Friday I staked out the bathroom for at least an hour. Up in my attic, I put on a bit of makeup—then a bit more. I nearly passed out hanging upside down to blow-dry my hair, but I reckoned the root lift was worth it. Then I put on my dress and my three silver rings and faced my reflection and—well, I thought I looked all right.

Dad gave me a lift to Art's house, and Fran opened the door to me, looking fabulous and a bit flushed. She was wearing very complicated earrings that jingled as she moved.

"Colette, *darling! Lovely* to see you! Come in, come in!" She swooped forward and kissed me on both cheeks. I tried not to seize up in surprise.

Er, had I missed something here? Had I slept through a couple of months of bonding and relationship forming? Fran was treating me like I was an old and cherished friend and I'd only been to her house once before. Mind you, they lived in the fast lane, Art's lot.

Maybe two visits qualified you as one of the family.

"You look heavenly," she trilled. "You young people never need to dress up to look good—it's so unfair." I was just trying to work out how big an insult that was when she shrieked, "*Art!* Where *is* he? Honestly, he's hopeless."

Art appeared in the hall, glowering. Then he saw me and his face opened up a bit. He was wearing some kind of jacket. Someone must have forced him into it at knifepoint, I thought.

"Get Colette a drink, darling," Fran said, and sailed off.

"You told me to wear *jeans!*" I hissed.

He grinned. "So?"

"So I'd have felt *completely* out of place!"

"You'd have looked great. You look OK in that dress thing, too. Come on."

We went into the kitchen and he poured us both out a huge glass of champagne. "Get ratted," he said. "It's the only way to get through this evening."

Suddenly Ian shoved his head around the kitchen door and barked, "Art—get IN there! NOW!" and disappeared. Art swore, then together we made our way to the living room.

I was quaking as I went around the door. The room seemed to be packed with glamorous, confident people, all screaming compliments at each other.

"Ah, here they are," said Ian. "This is Colette, everyone, Art's new girlfriend!"

Everyone turned to look at us, and I smiled—broadly. So I was Art's girlfriend, was I?

A little crowd gathered round, welcoming us. My smile felt welded to my face. Art was patted and kissed and punched playfully, and people made gruesome comments like "Not into Lego anymore then, young man?" Art looked blank throughout. Occasionally he said something or smiled, but he managed to look blank while he did it.

"You really hate this, don't you?" I whispered, when everyone drifted away.

"Yes I bloody do," he hissed back.

But I was beginning to relax a bit. I was fascinated, watching everyone. They all worked so hard at being animated and amusing, all doing their bit to create the evening. It was like an orchestra, harmonizing together. They all knew the score.

Then Fran called us all into dinner, to a huge white-clothed table glittering with shiny cutlery and candles and glasses. Ian jovially manhandled Art into a seat on the opposite side to me. I was on my own. I glanced over at Art and shrugged, smiling, but he wouldn't respond.

With a flourish, Fran plonked a huge platter on the table. "Antipasti, everyone, help yourselves!" she caroled. "You know us—no formality!"

The woman opposite me leaned over and said, "Now tell me, how did you two lovebirds meet?"

Cringing, I replied, "Swimming. At the local pool."

This caused shrieks of merriment around the table.

"How *healthy*," exclaimed the man next to Fran. "Mind you, I hear health clubs are the place to meet people these days." And he leered at Art.

Art looked back coldly. "We went there to swim," he said. "We met by accident."

More laughter. "That how you saw it, Colette?" the man continued. "Or did you have designs on our young man, eh? Bumping into him in the fast lane, eh?" This was so horribly near the truth that I went red.

Fran started topping up glasses, handing round crusty bread. The noise level was rising. There was a real atmosphere of pleasure, of indulgence—I don't know, it was different. Different to dinner at my house, that's for sure. I thought they were idiots in a way, talking inconsequential nonsense, but I liked it, too. The way they talked just for fun. After a while I even managed to put in a few words myself, and got drawn into a couple of conversations. I was doing OK, I thought.

Opposite me, Art sat there like stone. The woman next to him had given up trying to get him to talk. The minute we'd finished dessert, Art stood up. "Let's go, Coll," he said.

"Art, we haven't had *coffee* yet," wailed Fran.

"I don't want coffee," he said.

"Well, maybe Colette does," Fran hissed.

I'd have loved a cup, but I wasn't going to argue.

"I'm fine," I said politely, "really." Then as I stood up I said, "Thank you for a lovely meal."

I followed Art through the kitchen, where he grabbed an open bottle of wine from the table, and into the conservatory at the back. He slumped down on a sofa and took a deep glug from the bottle. "Thank God that's over."

"It wasn't *that* bad," I answered. "You'll have to come to my house. Then you'll appreciate all this."

"I don't think so," he answered. "Anyway, your mum looked bloody frightening."

"She is frightening," I said. "She's *terrifying*."

He wouldn't say any more, not even when I invited him to lighten up, so I stood up and wandered around the conservatory, admiring all the tropical plants. Then I stopped. On the wall was a picture frame with loads of photos stuck in it, one of those collagey things. Lots of Fran looking gorgeous, and lots of Fran and Ian looking smoochy, and one of Art. Holding hands with a girl with blond hair. It must have been taken on holiday or something, because they both looked tanned and she had the briefest of tops on.

I felt sick. It was a lovely photo. It had this envy-making atmosphere about it, and the girl looked so confident and much more beautiful than me. It suddenly flooded into me that it wouldn't work out with Art and me, it couldn't. I just wasn't in his league. Sooner or later he'd meet up again with the girl in the photo, or someone just like her, and I'd be ditched, sent back to my old life.

"Who's this?" I asked, once I could make my voice sound careless rather than choked.

He came and stood beside me. "Oh, God," he said. "I didn't know Fran'd put that up. That's Caroline."

He didn't say any more, and I couldn't ask. We heard the sounds of everyone leaving the dining room, laughing and exclaiming. "They're going back to the front room," Art said. Then he put his arms around me and we started kissing, and the feeling from the photo faded a bit.

## N O . 3 2

**A**rt did see me home in the car that night, but it wasn't a limo and anyway snogging on the back seat's a bit embarrassing with a driver right in front of you.

Around midday Saturday, as soon as I'd got up, I phoned him. I spoke to Fran first, and thanked her for a great evening. She was really friendly to me. In fact she was a lot nicer than Art, when he finally got on the phone. He sounded distinctly fed up. He's a moody sod, I thought to myself. Maybe he's just got a hangover.

We talked about seeing each other that night, but pretty halfheartedly. Art wanted to meet up with Mark, the idiot with the waistcoat and the men-only-club laugh. His reason was that we were both broke and Mark always had a stacked wallet. I wasn't keen at all— I thought it was pretty exploitative to use Mark like that, although I didn't exactly say so to Art. But I did say I'd put Mark right at the top of my list of People Not To Spend Time With. When I suggested we meet up at one or the other's house, though, Art got quite angry. "I just want to get *out*," he said. "I've had enough of it all—I've got to get out." So I backed down, and agreed to meet him later at one of the pubs on the old side of town.

Despite this, and despite knowing Mark would be there, I arrived at the pub in fairly high spirits. I felt pleased with myself for coping with last night's dinner, and fitting in OK. I was looking forward to having a laugh with Art about it. But it didn't turn out like that. No way.

Art was already sitting at a table with Mark when I walked into the bar. He barely managed to look up and say hello, let alone kiss me when I sat down next to him. When Mark went to get me a drink I asked him what was up, and the cold way he said, "Nothing. Should there be?" put me off asking any more. We both just sat there, silent.

Ten minutes later, to make things worse, Sally—the pale puffy blond who'd been with Pete at the Schroedinger gig—turned up. She seemed to be going out with Mark now, having ditched Pete, or poisoned him, or something. Well, all I can say is she and Mark deserved one another.

The evening got steadily worse. Mark happily paid for all the drinks; he seemed to think it was an honor that Art wanted to spend time with him on any terms. I found that pretty depressing: even complete idiots should have some pride. Sally still acted as though she didn't like me, and Art acted as though he didn't like anyone, including me. He just sat there, barely saying a word, staring at the three of us with a horrible, cold, appraising sneer on his face. I felt like crying. It was like a great barrier had come down between us, and I had no idea why.

Looking back, I feel almost ashamed that I didn't get straight to my feet and walk out of the pub. I hated how Art was behaving; I hated how he spent time with people he despised and showed he despised. I hated Mark and Sally—the way Mark blethered on inanely and the way Sally kept directing little smirks and comments at Art. I hated the whole evening and I didn't want to be there. But I stayed sitting where I was, and I felt diminished. A little cold feeling of dread was beginning to spread inside me.

He's going off you, I told myself. He's going to finish with you. And a pathetic desire to somehow elicit some kindness from him came over me. It was horrible.

Not long after that, Art said he had to go, and we all stood up. The miserable, panicky feeling grew inside me. Mark announced that he was getting a cab home, and he'd drop us all off—me first, because I wasn't out in the rich bit of town like the three of them. I longed for Art to say he'd walk with me, for some time on our own, but he said nothing, and neither did I.

When the cab arrived, Sally somehow managed to worm herself in between Art and me. As we drove along, I could hear her giggling things to him. I was in tears by this time, but it was dark and no one could see. When the driver drew up outside my house, I shot out before the cab had really stopped, mumbling, "Bye, thanks, Mark, bye." Halfway up the path I heard Art shouting "Hey, Coll!" and I looked back and saw him emerging from the far side of the cab. I muttered "see you" then I turned away and let myself in the front door.

Three hours later I was still awake. I lay in bed hopelessly depressed, convinced we were finished. I went over and over in my mind what had happened, trying to figure out why he'd changed. He'd been fed up at that stupid dinner the night before, but he'd still liked me. But tonight he'd completely shut down. I was frightened by how frightened I felt. I don't think I can stand feeling like this, I thought. It hurts too much.

On Sunday morning I phoned Val and went round to see her. I couldn't be completely honest with her, though. She was just beginning to accept Art, and I knew if I told her everything about last night she'd go straight back to thinking he was arrogant and spoiled. Part of me was beginning to agree with her.

So instead I just told her we'd had a bad night, and I was worried because he seemed to have cooled off.

"Look," she said firmly. "He sounds like a real moody sod to me. He was not *cool* about you at that party. He was anything but cool. You've just had a duff night, that's all. Don't take it personally."

Then I went on to tell her about Sally, how she seemed to have a thing about Art. Val shrugged. "Explains why she looked like she hated you, I suppose. But come on, Coll! You don't really think you've got any competition from *her*, do you?"

I cheered up a bit then, and she told me about her Saturday—how she'd been on a long hike with Greg, and a rather chilly picnic. I assumed at the time that a group of them had all gone out together, but she didn't actually say that. Then she said she was fixing something up for Wednesday night. I was half-hoping she'd ask me, too, because I could have done with seeing my old friends again. Particularly Greg. Someone who wasn't afraid to show he liked me and wouldn't suddenly turn strange on me. But she didn't ask me, and something stopped me from just inviting myself. In the old days, I wouldn't have hesitated, but it was different now, somehow. Maybe because I wasn't really one of the group anymore.

That night as I stacked the dishwasher, I brooded again about Art and Sally, and Art and Caroline and Art and all the other girls he'd probably made it with. I felt so inadequate. Such a beginner. No, not even a beginner—a non-starter.

When I'd finished, I went through into the living room. Mum was there, listening to some of her old rock tapes from the sixties. She was nodding her head to the beat and getting angry at the same time. She was really enjoying herself.

"Listen to those lyrics!" she exclaimed indignantly, as soon as I sat down. "That dreadful portrayal of women! Passive dolls supposed to bring any man who fancied them to the peaks of sexual frenzy, and still be insecure enough to ask 'Was I all right?' afterward! This really is man's music!"

The thought of Mum asking any man "Was I all right?" was enough to give me the giggles. "So why are you playing it, Mum?" I asked.

In answer she snorted, and slotted another tape into the machine. The Doors' "Light my Fire" came on, quite good to listen to, but more of the same. Jim Morrison telling his girlfriend to get more passionate, take him higher, light his fire. Listening to it made me even more depressed.

As far as Art was concerned, I'd only just about opened the box of matches.

## NO. 33

**B**y Wednesday I'd heard nothing from Art, and on Wednesday evening I phoned him and told him I had to give swimming a miss the next day. I don't really know why I did it. Partly because I felt we needed breathing space, but mostly because I was scared of experiencing a repeat of last Saturday.

He was really off with me on the phone. He acted like he couldn't care one way or the other, and we barely even said good-bye properly.

Things were not going well.

I lay up in my room for hours after I'd phoned him, not doing my homework, looking out of the skylight as the light faded. I don't want to want him a lot more than he wants me, I thought. It gave him too much power. A moody git like that shouldn't have power over anyone.

On Thursday, at the end of school, I was among the last few stragglers to leave the classroom. As I was walking out, Val called me back.

"Coll," she said. "Coll, look, I've got something to tell you."

She looked different, as she said that, serious, older, and she sounded very different. A feeling of dread started in the pit of my stomach. Somehow I knew this was about her and Greg.

"Look, Greg and I—you know we've been spending more time together?"

I nodded. Frozen.

"Well, we've—we've started going out together."

I just looked at her. I couldn't speak.

"It kind of . . . happened," she went on. "I mean, it started at that party."

"It's a bit *sudden*, isn't it?" I said, croakily. I don't know why it hit me so hard. I didn't know what to think.

"Oh, I know," she said. She seemed grateful that I'd even spoken. "I know it is. But we've always got on well, and I—I don't know, it's just amazing, it's—"

All of a sudden I couldn't help myself. I started to cry. Big, fat teardrops ran down my face.

"Coll! Coll, what is it?" Val sounded stricken. "I didn't think you'd be this upset. I mean, I know you like him, but you've got Art, and . . ."

I was glad for the tears. I let them come. They washed away all the hateful feelings. The jealousy, and the anger, and wanting to say "He's only with you because he couldn't have me!" and the sense of loss, the feeling that I was really on my own, now . . .

Val put her arms around me and I croaked out, "Look, I'm *glad* for you. I really am, underneath this, honestly!"

I sort of sagged down on the top of a desk, and she perched next to me and put an arm around me and rocked me, and after a while I could speak properly again. "I just don't know how it's working out with Art. I haven't seen him since Saturday. And I hardly *know* him, anyway. He's so closed off—and he's got this really nasty side. And Greg is so *kind* and *nice* . . . oh, I wish I'd really fancied him!" And I was off again, blubbing. "Art's had half the girls in England, anyway. I'm nothing special."

Val was still rocking me. "Yes, you are," she said. "Yes, you are."

"He'll probably finish with me when I next see him," I wailed.

"Coll, of course he won't. I saw you together at that party, remember! Of course he won't."

"Anyway, he's not kind like Greg," I sniveled. "Greg is *lovely*."

"Come on, Coll. Art's a complete kneetrembler. He's the one you want, not Greg." She was sounding a bit possessive already, I thought. I couldn't blame her.

I sat up and wiped my eyes. "I'm pleased for you, honestly, both of you," I said. "I'm just jealous, too."

"Coll, it's going to work out with you and Art, I know it is. And I can't believe you're jealous. We're still your friends."

"It won't be the same. You're a couple now. It won't be the same in the group." What I meant was, it won't be the same for me.

"Well, it wasn't the same when you went off with Art, was it?" Val replied. "Things don't stay the same, Coll. They've got to move on, or they stagnate."

We walked home together, and I tried to make an effort to be cheerful and not so self-centered about what had happened. Then, after I'd said good-bye to her, all the horrible feelings crowded in again. I had lots of mean little critical thoughts about how they'd rushed into things, but I knew the thoughts were unfair. Greg and Val had been close for years. It was Art and I who were like strangers.

I made myself face the fact that I'd always seen Greg as a last resort, as someone to fall back on, which was pretty shitty of me, but I'd still done it. I felt awful knowing he was with Val now. No more dates. Maybe even talking with him wouldn't be the same anymore.

Well, you're stuck on the wild side now, I thought. They're together, and you're out in the cold on your own. With someone you don't really trust. Who you don't know where you stand with. Who you want so much it scares you silly.

Then I climbed up to my attic, pulled the ladder up after me, and sobbed my heart out for half an hour. I felt I owed that to myself.

At school on Friday I acted really normal and cheerful, because I couldn't bear for Val to suspect what was going on underneath. That meant, of course, that I couldn't talk to her about Greg or Art or what I was going through, and that meant I felt even worse. I wanted to talk to her, but anything I said now would sound like regret over Greg.

Friday night came round, and I was at a real loss. There was no way I was phoning Art, and going out with everyone would mean having to look at Greg and Val, all dewy eyed and in love. So I stayed in. It was a long night.

Art finally phoned at about six on Saturday night. From his first hello, I could tell his mood had changed. And my depression lifted like a switch being thrown on a dark place. He didn't mention the awful night we'd had last Saturday, or our miserable phone conversation. But he sounded conciliatory, and he suggested going out. I felt a bit smug, as well as happy, as if I'd won some kind of game. Maybe me canceling swimming had made him sit up and take notice.

"I'm still broke, though," he said. "Five days of abject poverty to get through. They won't give me an advance."

"Oh, you materialist," I said, cheerfully. "We don't need money. Let's just wander about in town. And I've got enough to buy you a drink. One drink."

We met in town at around eight. It was great to see him again, and smiling, not all moody and withdrawn as he had been. We walked and walked, arms around each other. We had fun looking at all the other Saturday nighters: the lads on the make, the groups of dressed-up girls, the little rows going on, the disappointments, the pleasure. When we felt we'd earned it, we went into a pub and I went up to the bar to get two halves of lager.

"Make it last!" I said, as I sat down beside him. "I've got precisely 25p left!" I wanted to ask him why he'd been so moody, but somehow I didn't dare. Later, I told myself, maybe we can talk later. It was nice just to feel on an even keel again. I sat as close to him as I could get, feeling the warmth of his leg against mine.

After the pub, we stopped under some trees. It felt so right, kissing; we were hungry for each other. After a while he pulled back and said, "Why did you rush off like that on Saturday?"

"Why did . . .? You were the one behaving like a complete prat all night."

"Oh, I was just a bit pissed off . . ."

**166**

"*Just a bit pissed off?* If that was just a bit pissed off, I'd hate to spend time with you when you're a lot pissed off."

"OK, OK, you superior cow. Look, I didn't mean to upset you. It wasn't about you."

"You didn't upset me," I said quickly.

"Yes I did. You wouldn't even kiss me good-bye."

"Well, what was I supposed to do—climb over Sally to get at you?"

He laughed. "Oh, right. Sally. She's a drag."

"You can say that again. But you've slept with her, haven't you?"

"I went out with her for a few weeks, last year. It was bad."

"And you slept with her." I had to ask. It was like picking a scab.

He shrugged. "A couple of times."

I felt cold. He made it sound so unimportant.

"Don't look at me like that," he said. "You've done stupid things, too, haven't you?"

There was a pause, and then I asked, "Well, what *were* you pissed off about?"

"Oh, everything. That phony carnival Dad and Fran made us go through. That dinner. And seeing you playing along with it—"

"Oh, come *on*. I was just being polite. I could hardly sit there and sulk like you did, could I?"

He smiled. "Maybe not. I just—I just hate being

**167**

around them sometimes. Fran and the old man. I get psychotic—really nasty. Maybe you shouldn't get tied up with me."

For a moment I felt chilled again. Then I gave him a shove and said, "Oh, stop being so melodramatic, you jerk."

For some reason, that seemed to cheer him up immensely. He swore at me, and laughed, and then we started necking again. It's too late, anyway, I thought. I'm tied up with you already. After a while he said, "Listen, why don't I come to your place tomorrow?"

I was delighted he'd asked, but a bit alarmed, too. What would he think of it, after his palatial home? "You're kidding!" I said. "I thought you were too frightened of my mum?"

"You'll protect me. Even if you don't, it's better than being at my place. Will your folks mind? Have they got anything on?"

"They've never got anything on," I said. "It'll be fine."

"I'll come round about three? We could go out for a walk or something. At least it makes you fit, being broke."

When I let myself in that night, I looked around me, trying to see the house with new eyes, like Art would see it tomorrow. There was no way around it, the place was a dump. I wandered into the living room and told Mum

**168**

that Art was coming round tomorrow, if that was OK.

She peered at me over her tortoiseshell reading glasses. "So we're going to MEET him at last, are we?" she said. "I'll look forward to it. He must be quite exceptional if he's so totally replaced Greg in your affections."

"Justine!" murmured Dad as I left the room in despair. Not a good omen for tomorrow. And if I'd hoped my mention of Art's visit might make Mum flick a duster around, I was seriously out of luck.

# NO. 35

hoovered round the hall and living room next morning, and then started on the kitchen. Mum came in just as I was scrubbing at the table.

"Oh, for GOODNESS sake," she spat. "What *has* come over you? Why this sudden obsession with HOUSEWORK?" She said the word in the way other mothers would say GLUE SNIFFING.

"It's not an obsession. I'm just cleaning the table. Well, wiping it. It would take a sandblaster to get it clean."

"Oh, ha ha. It's that boy you've asked round, isn't it? Who is he anyway? Some nasty little sub-editor on *House Beautiful* magazine? Think he'll go off you if he can't eat his dinner off the toilet seat?"

"Look, Mum, I often clean up. Just leave it, will you," I said.

"Oh, rubbish. You do NOT often clean up. You're still clinging to this nuclear family idea that I ought to be doing it all because I'm your MOTHER. You're doing it to impress this little tyke you've asked round, aren't you? Admit it! You want him to think you have a gracious home life. You'll be arranging the fruit bowl next."

Which was funny, because just before she'd come in I had ditched a couple of rotting bananas and a moldy peach from the fruit bowl in an attempt to upgrade it a little. But it still didn't manage to look arranged, exactly.

After I'd done the table I gave up, and went upstairs to get changed. At least my room is beautiful, I thought. I was looking forward to showing Art that. It might not have the graciousness of his home, but it had my stamp on it.

Not long after three, the doorbell went. I ran to answer it, and there he was, grinning and gorgeous on the doorstep. I wanted to kiss him hello, but Mum's presence in the kitchen inhibited me. I stepped back, and Art came inside. He was only a couple of inches away from me but he could have been behind an electric fence for all the accessibility I felt. It was really weird seeing him in my home setting. Better get the Confrontation over with, I thought, and I led him to the kitchen.

If this had been a film, now would have been when the low, threatening music started up. Mum was seated in her place of authority at the end of the table, surrounded by papers. When she saw us come in she leaned forward slightly, placed her hands flat on the table in front of her, squared her shoulders, and surveyed Art. He came to a standstill, drew himself up to his six-foot-something, and surveyed her.

I had this extraordinary feeling that they were a match for each other. They were like creatures in some ancient arena, taking stock. And I knew as I watched that they hated each other on sight.

"WELL!" said Mum, in a voice even louder than her usual one. "You must be ART!"

Art cracked his face into a dazzling, phony smile and came toward her, stretching out his hand. "Mrs. Rowlands!" he replied. "I'm so pleased to meet you!"

Lying git, I thought, as I watched, fascinated. This was a side of Art I'd never seen before. He was making an effort. He was being . . . charming.

Mum, of course, was given no choice but to take his hand and pump it briefly, which gave him a slight advantage. But she was soon back on top.

"Art as in Art GARFUNKEL, hmm—?" she asked.

*Cringe.*

"Yes, well," Art replied, "Dad's generation, you know. I was christened Arthur."

"And you met Colette SWIMMING?" she shot back with a hostile, interrogatory air, as though she was waiting for him to break down and confess that he'd actually introduced himself by pulling me off my bike and into the bushes.

"That's right. Coll's a great swimmer. Really fit."

172

Mum's eyebrows shot up, as though he'd said something indecent. But she let it pass, and said, "Yes, it's important nowadays, fitness. I do all I can to encourage her."

*Although obviously not by example* hung in the air unspoken.

"That's great," said Art, after an awkward pause.

"Colette makes good use of that sports center," she went on.

*Oh no, not the self-defense classes, Mum. Please don't mention them.*

"Swimming a couple of times a week. And of course her . . ."

*PLEASE!*

"—self-defense classes."

Art turned to me, a slightly crowing look of delight on his face. "You didn't tell me you went to self-defense classes!" he said.

"Keeping them up her sleeve, I expect," said Mum, smugly. "Surprise being a strong ingredient of attack."

"Attack?" asked Art, innocently. "I thought this was defense."

Mum was nettled. You could see she was dying to say "Don't you get smart with me, my lad!" Instead she said, "Sometimes it can amount to the same thing. You'll have a coffee, won't you?" and went to put the kettle on.

"So when do you go to these self-defense classes?" Art asked me.

**173**

"Every Monday," answered Mum from the sink, like I was three years old again.

"I've been going for two years now," I said, quickly. "The teacher's very good."

Art was smiling lecherously. "I really like strong women," he said.

*Dong!!!* That sort of comment might be par for the course in Art's home, but here it was taboo. The way he'd said it, you knew he was thinking of some swarthy female chucking him backward onto a bed. You could tell Mum was feeding it through her Geiger counter checking for sexist fallout, and it was setting off high-level alarms.

She turned to face him, coffee jar in hand. "And why is that, particularly?" she asked, a little too pleasantly.

All Art's expensive education had obviously been to some good. He saw the danger signs and executed a perfect verbal backflip. "Ah, well, you know, I really hate all that Victorian belittling of women we've inherited. That women are frail and weak. The female physiognomy is not all that different from the male's—the muscle groupings and so on. Women can have enormous strength and endurance, almost as much as men."

Mum was staring at him as he came to a standstill. Her eyes were narrowed. She couldn't really fault anything that he'd said, which must have been pretty disappointing for her. "GREATER than men, sometimes," she said. "Look at childbirth."

**174**

*Oh, no, Mum, please! Let's please not look at childbirth!*

I held my breath. Mum has a vast catalog of birthing horror stories, all perfect for freaking out a new boyfriend. But even Mum knows when to call it quits. She turned away and finished making the coffee. "Here you are, then," she said, slamming two mugs down in front of us. "I'll leave you two to it."

We sat down dumbly at the table. Art's mug had a picture of an angry-looking woman holding a gun, and the words *So many men, so few bullets* underneath.

"You're right about how different your lot are," he said, shaking his head slightly.

I bridled. "You mean we don't have a cappuccino machine?" I was feeling a bit defensive about the instant coffee. And the mug.

"Don't be daft! I mean, it's . . . bohemian. Intellectual. Content not form, you know. She's a real old hippie, your mum, isn't she? Left-wing as hell."

"I can't argue with that," I said. Well, I couldn't.

"She doesn't like me much," he added.

*Understatement of the year.* "She doesn't like *anyone* male much," I replied. "Don't take it personally. Hurry up and finish that coffee. I want to show you my attic."

I was dying to show him my new room. Mind you, last night, as I was going to bed, Mum had had one of her little chats with me. "It's fine to show your-young-man the loft, Colette," she'd said. "But I want you to leave the hatch open and the steps down. Is that clear?"

**175**

It was clear. I didn't even bother to ask why. She wanted to be able to thunder up the ladder at the first sound of any sexual activity and aim a fire extinguisher at us.

We emptied our mugs and went into the hall. Mum and Sarah were just coming downstairs.

"I'm going to show Art the loft, Mum, OK?" I said.

"Fine," she said, giving me a look heavy with renewed warning. As we walked up the stairs I could hear Sarah squeaking, "But what does he want to go out with Colette for, Mum? He's ever so good-looking."

Later, I thought. You can kill her later.

We pulled down the ladder and climbed up. Art loved the place. He walked round and round, looking out of the skylight, falling backward on the bed, sitting on the cushions next to the railings.

"This is great," he kept saying. "I wish I had somewhere like this. So far away from everyone." He walked back to the hatch. "And the stairs just sort of slide up, do they? You pull them up after you?"

There was nothing for it, I had to tell him.

"Er, Art," I said. "Mum's made me promise to leave the stairs down if you're up here. It's kind of like those old black and white films they made in the 1930s. They could only have a bed scene if the man kept one foot on the floor. To show they weren't doing it. We've got to keep the ladder on the floor. To show we're not."

Art looked confused and sleazy at the same time. "I don't see how having a foot on the floor shows you're not doing it. It's quite easy to . . ."

"Oh, shut up," I said.

# NO. 36

**L**ater we went for a walk. The weather was cold and gray, but as we sauntered along hand in hand, I felt great. Walking, I matched his pace like I did in the pool, or on our bikes. We headed out of town and this time, Art started the conversation.

"You've got a real traditional family, haven't you? I mean, you're a real part of your family."

"Well, yes," I said. "Why wouldn't I be?"

He shrugged, and was silent for a minute. Then he said, "Your mum keeps tabs on you, doesn't she?"

"Yes. Big ones. Iron-studded ones."

"Shows she cares, I suppose."

"Shows she—! You sound like my dad. She's just nosy as hell."

He turned and grinned at me. "That's why you're so virtuous."

I quickened my pace. "I don't think I'm particularly virtuous. Just . . ."

"Just what?"

"Just discriminating," I answered, and he laughed, and hugged me to him.

It's all right again, I thought, as we walked on. It's going to be all right.

When we got back, Mum emerged from the kitchen, swathed in a huge checked pinny. "We're just about to eat," she pronounced. "Arthur? You're very welcome to join us."

"*Art!*" I hissed. "He's called *Art!*"

"Thank you, Mrs. Rowlands," he said. "I'd love to."

You wouldn't say that if you'd tasted Mum's cooking, I thought. But I was pleased he wanted to stay. And I was quite touched Mum had asked him.

"I thought you'd had a big Sunday lunch," I said to him, as Mum returned to the stove.

"I've walked it all off. What's the matter—want to get rid of me?" In answer I risked a quick neck by the stairs. Dangerous action, with Mum only next door.

Soon we were all sitting around the kitchen table, contemplating the flabby-looking lasagna that Mum had plonked in the middle. But dinner turned out to be surprisingly pleasant, mainly because Art turned out to know quite a bit about architecture. He'd done some sort of course on it, and he asked all these questions that Dad found interesting.

Art seemed really relaxed—even Sarah's unblinking stare didn't faze him. I wasn't relaxed, though. It was

**179**

weird, having him sit at our table. I knew what Mum was thinking: to her, Art was privileged, slick, and far too sure of himself. I knew she hated him.

I couldn't resist challenging her about it later, after he'd gone. After I'd seen him all the way to the gate and we'd kissed for ages by the holly tree. I don't want all this disapproval simmering beneath the surface, I thought. Let's get it out in the open.

"OK, tell me," I said, aggressively, cornering her in the kitchen. "You think he's awful and not a patch on Greg. You think I'm mad to be seeing him and not Greg. You think I'd be a lot better off with Greg." I planned to tell her exactly what Greg was up to nowadays when she said yes, and take the wind out of her sails.

She looked at me, then said carefully, "Yes, but it's not as simple as that, is it, Colette? You don't . . ."—she searched for the right word—"fancy Greg. You do fancy Art. You make that painfully obvious every time you open your mouth or look at him. And that makes all the difference in the world."

I gawped at her. I'd been expecting her to say something along the lines of "Gregory-is-a-very-nice-young-man-worth-ten-of-that-oversexed-overindulged-overrated-Arthur-or-Art-as-he-pretentiously-calls-himself." Instead she was actually acknowledging the power of sexual attraction. I also felt a bit embarrassed. How on earth had I been acting, to give so much away?

"Don't GAWP at me like that," Mum said, bridling a

little. "I do know about magnetism, sexual chemistry, you know. Weird, alien, and obscene as it may seem to you, young lady, I haven't been like this all my life."

She made a sweeping gesture that seemed to take in the mess in the kitchen sink and the family laundry piled in the hall. So it was true, then. Back sometime when Tyrannosaurus Rex had ruled the earth, Mum had felt fruity. I felt a little queasy at the thought.

But I had to admit it made sense. She was still a passionate woman. That's why people were drawn to her. It's just that now she seemed to direct her passion against men, instead of toward them. And she didn't appear to direct much of anything toward Dad.

She seemed to read my thoughts. "What drew your father and I together is exactly what's drawing you to Art," she announced. And with that, she left the room— without even giving me her usual warning about being careful, taking it slow. I felt pleased, hopeful somehow. Maybe it was OK to feel so blown away, so obsessed. In a funny way, I felt as though Mum had just given her blessing to the whole relationship.

# NO. 37

I was hyper that week. All I wanted to do was see Art, but he had some kind of mock exams on and couldn't get away until Friday. By Wednesday night I was cracking at the seams. I knew I wouldn't get to sleep if I didn't work off some of my excess energy.

Around ten, I put on my running gear and slipped out of the house quietly, so Mum wouldn't hear me go. She thinks it's "asking for trouble" to run that late. The mood I was in, I couldn't have cared less what trouble came my way. I'd bounce straight off it.

I set off on my usual route, around the big block away from the main road, and along toward the park. I was running faster than usual and by the time I got to the lane that runs along the park boundary, I'd got cramp in my leg. I stopped, put my hands flat on a tree trunk and started stretching my leg out, easing the muscle. As I stretched, I could hear someone talking. It was coming from the trees on the other side of the railings, inside the park.

"Come on, darling, what's the matter? Don't go all cold on me now." A man. He sounded drunk.

Then I heard a panicky voice saying something in return. Pleading. Oh, God, I thought, that sounds nasty. I stood quietly, listening.

"You weren't like this in the club, were you? Friendly enough then, ay?" and then there was the sound of some movement, and some more from the pleading voice, louder this time. Didn't I know that voice, the girl's voice?

"Come on, stop mucking me around. You want it, too," I heard, and then from the girl, "Look, I just want to go home, OK? Just let me go!"

Then it struck me. I did know the voice. It was Tricia!

"Tricia?" I called out, loudly. "Tricia? Are you all right?" Maybe knowing someone was there would put him off.

"Piss off," came the man's voice.

"She don't need your help," came another man's voice.

There were two of them! Without really thinking, I shot to the railings, and heaved myself up. I crouched at the top for a second, balancing, then jumped down into the park. I landed right next to the three of them, and they all spun around to face me. Oh, shit. My stomach contracted with fear. I've done it now, I thought.

"Bloody 'ell, who d'you think you are—Batman?"

said one of the men. He had his hands on Tricia's elbows, holding her to him.

"Come to join us, have you?" said the other one.

"Tricia, are you all right?" I said, loudly.

She looked at me, panic-stricken. "He won't let me go!" she wailed.

"Let her go," I shouted. "She wants to go home."

"Don't you bloody well tell *me* what to do," said the man holding her.

"Just let her go! Get your hands off her!"

The other man was walking toward me. "Don't get so noisy, darlin'," he was saying, in a slurred voice. "Why don't you just come and join us, eh?"

He got hold of my arm.

I automatically jerked it free, just like we'd been taught in class and the man staggered to one side.

"Getting nasty, eh?" He lurched around to face me, fists clenched. "You little cow." I gazed back at him, frozen.

He came at me again and grabbed me, twisting me around, hitting my face against a tree. I had this wavering, unreal feeling with the pain. Not to me, I thought, this can't happen to me! Suddenly a huge surge of adrenaline pumped through my veins and, driven by fear and hatred, I gave him the works. I stamped down hard on the instep of his foot, smashed my fist backward into his groin, then brought it back up, hard, into his face. He fell, groaning.

The other man had let go of Tricia and was heading straight for me. "You bitch . . ." he bellowed, grabbing at me.

My arms shot up in front of my face and knocked his arms away. I brought my fist hard up into his nose. Then I kneed him in the groin and brought my elbow sharp down onto the back of his neck as he fell forward. I jumped backward to get out of his way—I could hear him retching.

Behind the fear I felt a wild elation. Sonia, my teacher! It works! It works!

"RUN!" I screamed at Tricia. "RUN!"

She was rooted to the spot, terrified. I seized her arm and charged through the trees, pulling her along beside me.

"Get rid of those stupid shoes," I shouted, and she kicked off her high heels. I thought I could hear movement behind me. I ran faster, dragging her along, too.

Then I remembered the Voice—a woman's best weapon. "HELP! We're being CHASED!" I screamed. "HELP US!"

We crashed out onto open space. Scanning the park desperately, I spotted a man with a dog on the other side of the grass. "HELP!" I screamed, loud enough to rip my throat. "HELP US!"

Thankfully this man was not the sort of citizen you read about, the sort who walks on by and pretends nothing has happened. He turned and began to run

**185**

toward us, his dog bounding beside him. "What's going on?" he shouted.

"Men!" I yelled. "Men chasing us!"

He reached us, and his dog raced into the trees, barking. I risked a look around, and saw nothing. They'd gone. We'd got away. I took a great, shuddering breath of air deep into my lungs. Adrenaline coursed through me like an electric current.

The dog came bounding back. Shakily, I told the man what had happened. He listened, concerned and angry, then he said he'd see us home. Tricia was sobbing, and saying things like "my Dad'll kill me" and "oh, Coll, you were so brave." I kept my arm around her shoulder as she hobbled along, shoeless.

We got to my house, and the man watched until he saw the front door open and let us inside.

# NO. 38

might have known that the minute Mum got involved, the whole drama would blow sky high. First we had to work hard to assure her we weren't hurt. Then we explained what had happened, and her face grew murderous. If she'd had a gun, I think she'd have gone right out and found those men and blown their heads off. She did the next best thing—she phoned the police and told Dad to make us some hot tea and brandy.

We all sat around the kitchen table, and Dad poured us out huge mugs of tea. Tricia took a gulp of hers and then started crying again when Mum said she had to phone her parents.

"They have to know you're safe, dear," Mum said firmly. "Tell me your number."

When Mum came back from the phone, Tricia launched into her story of what happened. "I was at that new club, with Sam," she whimpered. "We got talking to those two men—they seemed really nice. We were dancing and stuff, and they said they'd give us a lift home. They dropped Sam off first and then the guy I was sort of with said he wanted to go for a walk in the park and stopped the car. I got out, because I thought I'd better walk the rest of the way home, only he got hold of my arm and pulled me into the trees. He was trying to kiss me—I was really scared . . ." She started to cry again, and Mum stroked her hair. "Then I heard Coll calling out, and she jumped over the fence toward us. She was brilliant. One of the men went for her and she punched him in the face, and . . . and then the other one went for her, and she punched *him* and kneed him in the balls and we just ran, and I . . . I left my new shoes in the park." She dissolved into weeping again.

There was a silence. Had I really done all that? I could feel myself shaking; my hands trembled around my mug of tea. That routine, that old routine that Sonia made us practice again and again—it had saved us both. I looked down at my right hand. It hurt, and I could see a bruise beginning.

Dad put his arms around me. "You brave girl," he said. "If anything had happened to you, I don't know what I . . ." He stopped. He was crying, a little. Suddenly I was crying, too, crying with relief. All the horror of the last hour flooded out of me, as I let go of the fear. Dad held onto me, stroking my hair in silence, and I could hear Mum fussing and exclaiming next to us as though she was a long, long way away.

"I didn't really decide to do it," I sobbed. "It just sort of happened."

"TWO of them," Mum said. "You took on *two* of them."

"Oh, Mum, they were drunk slobs. Don't make a big thing of it. It was horrible."

She gathered me up from Dad's arms and hugged me, hard. "I know," she said.

That night seemed to go on and on. All the noise woke Sarah, and she came downstairs. She listened round-eyed while Dad explained what had happened, then she flew at me and hugged me, and I couldn't help it, I started crying again, with her sitting on my knee. Then Tricia's parents arrived, and after that the police came, and we sat drinking more tea while they took our statements, and then finally, everyone left. I was completely exhausted. Mum helped me up to bed, saying all the little soothing things she used to when I was scared of nightmares as a child. Before I knew it, I was out for the count.

When I woke up the room was very light and Mum was standing beside my bed with a cup of tea.

"Morning!" she said. "It's ten o'clock. You've had a wonderful sleep—best thing for you. How are you feeling?"

"All right, Mum. Honestly."

"Well, no school today—you rest. I've phoned your teacher."

I smiled at her, then turned onto my side and drank the tea. I still felt tired and wobbly, but it was weird, it was already starting to feel as though it had all happened to somebody else.

Mum spent most of the morning on the phone to members of the Sisterhood. I stood a good chance of being canonized as their patron saint, after what I'd done.

## NO. 39

That evening, early, I phoned Art, and told him what had happened. He sounded really shaken, and kept asking me if I was all right. Then he said, "Look, let's go out. Now. I want to see you."

I felt all sort of warm when he said that. "I suppose I could go out for a couple of hours after dinner—"

"I'll buy you dinner."

"But it's still not the end of the month. You're skint."

"I'll tell Fran what a hero you are and get some money out of her. I'll pick you up at eight, OK?"

At five to eight I was on my way downstairs when I heard Mum talking in a loud voice in the hall. And then I heard Art's voice, equally loud. I hung over the banister and listened, fascinated. Mum was telling Art how brave I'd been, and how I really shouldn't be going out so soon, because I needed time to get over it properly. Simultaneously, Art was telling Mum how brave I'd been, and how I needed to get out and put the whole incident behind me.

It was deadlock. What she really wanted to say was: "Get out of my house, you VILE boy!" And what he wanted to say was: "Butt out, you old battle-ax!" It was getting a bit heated, but I knew I could handle it.

"Hi, Art," I said, speeding down the stairs. "Mum, I'm going out."

"Colette! Is that wise? So soon after that ordeal . . ."

"Mum, I'm fine. Don't wait up. Bye!" And, kissing her on the cheek, I pushed Art through the door.

"Well, that was something!" he said, as soon as we were outside. "The way you handled that. She really is protective, your mum, isn't she?" Then he stopped and stared at me, and slowly put a hand up to the graze on my cheek.

"He hurt you," he said, almost expressionless. With one finger, he traced the outline of the graze. Then he pulled back suddenly, produced a bulging wallet out of his pocket, and waved it triumphantly in front of me. "So, where do you want to eat?"

"*Art!*" I was half impressed, half appalled. "How much did Fran *give* you? She did *give* it to you, didn't she?" I had visions of him rooting through her handbag.

"Yup," he answered. "Loads. And so did Dad."

"You went to *both* of them! You are *totally* without moral fiber!"

"Crap. They're both really concerned for you, that's all. They think you're wonderful. So do I. Now come on."

o    o    o

The evening that followed was the best yet. We held hands across the table, and ate off each other's plates, and he was more open, more relaxed, than he'd ever been. That awful Saturday night seemed like some twisted old dream now. He wanted to know every detail of my act of heroism, and seemed really concerned, and full of admiration.

"You're not put off then?" I said. "I'm not too macho for you?"

He laughed. "Nope. I told you—I like strong women."

"Yeah?" I pushed it.

He laughed. "Yeah. I hate twiggy little girls who look as though they'd fall over if they picked up a bag of sugar."

Then we ordered three puddings between us.

After the meal he walked me home, with lots of jokes about how really I should be seeing him home, and we stood for ages by the holly tree, talking and kissing. Neither of us wanted to say goodnight.

# NO. 40

The very next night Art phoned and asked me to go away with him that weekend. He laughed at my stunned silence. "We've got a cottage," he said, "In the country."

"You rich sods."

"OK, don't come if you feel principled about it. No—do come. You'll love it. There's loads of space. I mean, we'll have to put up with Fran and Dad doing their back-to-the-soil act, but it'll be worth it."

A cottage in the country. Lots of space, lots of time, and Art. "I . . . well, yes, I'd love to come!" I stuttered, delighted.

"We won't leave here until tomorrow lunchtime—Dad's got to work in the morning. And we'll have to come back on Sunday after lunch. It's not long enough, but it's not that far away and—it's good. It's so open: the sky is just amazing."

The *sky?* Art talking about the *sky?* Things were looking up. "Look, I'd love to come," I said. "I just have to get around Mum. I mean, she hasn't met your folks . . ."

"Want me to get Fran to phone her?"

"No," I said gravely, imagining what a conversation between Mum and Fran would be like, especially if Fran called Mum "darling." "I'll handle it. I'm sure I can come—I'll phone you back."

As soon as I put the phone down I hunted Mum out in her new office. She'd only moved in about a week ago and already it was jam-packed with files. You're going to have to bring this up very carefully, I told myself as I walked up to her desk. Be tactful. Ease her into it.

"Mum?" I said brightly. "Art's asked me to go away with him for the weekend . . ."

Well done, Coll. The explosion that followed only just avoided being reported on the six o'clock news. After a lot of handflapping and "Hear me *out!*"s, I finally got her to calm down enough to listen.

"Not on his *own*," I practically shouted at her. "God, Mum, what did you think? His *parents* will be there. His parents will be there *all* the time. It's their weekend cottage he's asked me to. They often ask people down."

Mum sniffed disparagingly. She still disapproved. "Weekend cottage indeed," she grumbled, "while some people sleep in cardboard boxes!"

"Mum, that is a political objection." I was pretty proud of myself for thinking up that one. "What *real* objections have you got?"

And Mum went fairly rapidly through her list. "You

**195**

hardly know him! A whole weekend when you hardly know him! You're getting too involved; in too deep too soon; you're only sixteen; there'll be plenty of time for all this kind of thing later; other priorities; concentrate on schoolwork; what happened to that nice group of friends you used to see . . ."

I let her rant her way to silence. Then I said, "But you're not going to stop me going, are you?" and Mum had to gloweringly agree that she wasn't.

Dad dropped me round at Art's place at about two on Saturday. He left me at the end of the drive. There was a tacit understanding between Art and me that there wasn't much point in our parents mixing. No common ground.

"Have fun, Colette," Dad said, as I got out of the car with my backpack. "Be careful. Be good!"

I knocked on the huge front door and, after a minute or so, Art opened it. We said hi, and Art leaned forward and kissed me. He was always so relaxed, so sure of himself. Well, I could be confident, too—outwardly, anyway. I reached up, drew him back down, and kissed him. He was grinning as we moved apart. I'm spending the night with him, I thought, excitedly. Well, sort of spending the night with him. I'll have breakfast with him, anyway.

From the kitchen I could hear sounds of crashing and swearing. "What's up?" I asked.

"Oh, the usual chaos. The old man is late—said he'd be back by one and he's still not here. Fran's packing up and cursing him. You'd better come and say hello to her."

The cooking island in the middle of the kitchen was covered in boxes of food and drink. Fran was consulting a long list as we went in. She swooped on me and kissed me on both cheeks.

"Colette, *darling!* I'm so glad you're here! Are you all right, sweetheart? Art told me—dreadful business, dreadful!" But before I could answer she got on to what really mattered. "I *still* haven't got everything ready! It's all a total mess, as you can see! Darling, can *you* help me with this—Art's completely *hopeless.* He'll eat it, but he won't help get it ready. Art, we'll check everything off and you can load it in the car. Do you think you can manage that, sweetie?"

"Yes, *sweetie,* I think I can," he said, as he walked out of the kitchen. "Call me when you're ready."

"Honestly, that *boy,*" she spat. "I don't know how you put up with him, darling, honestly I don't. Looks aren't everything, you know."

Coming from someone who spent at least an hour every morning getting dressed and made up, that was a bit rich, I thought. She handed me the list and I had to read it out as she flapped around making sure everything was there. She'd gone to a huge amount of trouble: *coq au vin* for this evening's meal already prepared,

**197**

nibbles and chocolates, cheeses and an apple flan, a great slab of lamb for Sunday—it was quite touching, in a way.

"It all looks wonderful, Fran, it really does," I said, soothingly. "It must have taken you ages."

"What? Oh, Colette, you are sweet. Those two *men* never notice. But they'd be up in arms if something was missing."

You need a consciousness raising session with my mum, I thought. She'd soon sort you out. Half an hour's lecture from her and you'd start telling them where to shove their canapés.

Twenty minutes later, we'd got it all packed up and Art was loading the Range Rover. Then Ian slammed into the drive in his little BMW convertible. Honestly, even their cars belonged in some smoothy lifestyle manual.

"I'm sorry! I'm sorry!" Ian bellowed as he scrambled out of the driver's seat and launched himself at Fran for an apologetic kiss. "Bloody phone call from the States just as I was leaving. All hell's breaking loose over there. Had to sort it out."

Fran had set her face into a tight little smile, sort of forgiving but not quite. Mum would have brained him, then deafened him. But Fran only said, "It's fine, Ian. The kids have helped."

"Super. Great stuff. Let's go. I'll just run in and change." He legged it into the house. Under Fran's

**198**

direction, we locked the back door and turned on the terrifying alarm system. Then we climbed in the Range Rover and Fran reversed it out of the drive.

After a few miles, everyone began to relax a bit, even Fran, and there was quite a festive feeling as we hit the motorway. Ian put some loud jazz into the tape machine at the front, and started massaging Fran's neck as she drove. She kept pivoting her neck backward, rubbing her cheek against his hand. Those two really are sensualists, I thought. No wonder Art's so physical. As I thought this he slid over the seat and wrapped his arms around me. We kept overtaking cars with normal people in them, people who kept to their own spaces and didn't constantly stroke and kiss each other. I felt luxuriously superior.

After an hour or so, Fran turned off the motorway and soon we were driving on country roads. Ian turned the jazz up even louder and started boogying about in his seat. Art laughed, and raised his eyes skyward. The mood in the car grew happier as the roads got narrower and the trees got thicker overhead.

"Nearly there, kids!" Ian said, jubilantly.

"There's a rabbit!" squealed Fran, as though she'd just spotted an alien species never before seen on Earth. "Look, by the side of the road!" The rabbit headed into the hedgerow, and the car bumped along a bit more slowly. Then Fran swerved neatly into a flagged parking space by an old, crumbling wall. We had arrived.

The silence as we got out of the car was wonderful. It kind of boomed around us. You could hear absolutely nothing: no traffic, no people, just a few birds breaking into the quiet now and then. But the greater surrounding silence remained. It was like outer space.

Everywhere you looked, there was just trees, and grass, and a huge, huge sky. Fran and Ian were gazing around them with soppy expressions on their faces. "It never fails us, does it," said Ian. "It's always marvelous."

We each took a box or bag from the boot, followed Ian up a little overgrown path and waited while he unlocked the front door. As he opened it, a hideous mechanical wailing ripped into the air, shattering the wonderful silence, making me jump.

Art laughed. "It's the alarm," he said. "Everything we own is alarmed."

Ian dived into the house and stuck his head into a cupboard, where he began frantically punching numbers into a keyboard. The wailing stopped abruptly.

"You have to turn it off within five seconds of opening the front door," Art continued, "or the machine guns and mustard gas capsules hidden in the ceiling are activated."

"Oh, ha, ha," said Ian, as he emerged from the cupboard. "You wait till you're paying the bills. You'll want protection then, my lad."

"Everything through in the kitchen, please!" said Fran brightly, and we dutifully followed her through the stone-flagged hall. I set my box down on the kitchen table and looked out of the window. All I could see was green. Some kind of creeper was even growing across the windowpane, trying to get into the house. The kitchen was filled with a lovely, watery pale green light.

We fetched the rest of the luggage as Fran filled up the fridge. I left my backpack under an old oak settle in the hall. I wasn't in any hurry to unpack.

"That's the last," said Art, staggering through the front door with a box full of bottles. "Dad's taken the sheets and stuff upstairs. I want to show Coll the land before it gets dark."

As we left the cottage, the clean air, the wind, hit us. We went past the pond at the end of the garden, and out through an old gate into the fields. We walked and walked, in silence, in rhythm. We didn't need to talk. As we went downhill our pace picked up. We went through the woods, then we climbed up to the old windmill, and circled it, peering in the windows at the massive grinding stones.

Then we set off again, toward the endless open.

# NO. 41

After a couple of hours we'd reached the top of a ridge, and we sat down on a log, near an ancient-looking little copse of trees. Art handed me an apple, and we sat munching.

"It's completely beautiful here," I said. "I bet outlaws used to live in those trees."

"Maybe," he said. "The trees used to cover the land once. Forest everywhere you looked."

"You are so lucky," I said, "having this place to come to."

He didn't answer.

The sun was setting. Below us, the wind was moving in a field of long grass, and as the grass swayed, the warm light played over it in undulating patterns. Constantly changing.

"Look at that," he said. "It's heaving. It's alive."

Suddenly this feeling kind of washed over me, a surging, waving feeling like the movement in the grass, and I felt so happy, it frightened me. I rolled backward off the log and lay on the grass, looking at the sky. And pretty soon, as I expected, Art's face was there, between me and the sky, and we were kissing.

Kissing is better in the open air. Art's mouth tasted of apple. He felt heavy and strong and warm.

I stroked the hair from his face and the wind blew it back again. Just to be alive, and here, I thought, is enough. I wound my arms around his neck, and we kissed again. All I could hear was the wind in the trees and our breathing.

After a while the weight of him, covering me, began to feel a bit overwhelming, and I wasn't sure if I wanted to feel that, so I shifted sideways and rolled around and on top of him. He started laughing. "You *strong woman*," he said. "I love *strong women!*" and then he tipped me over and underneath him again. We were both laughing now, a ragged excited sound, and he started kissing my neck, my ear, and then from behind us was another sound, a wet, frantic panting noise, and before my brain could work out what was happening a pair of huge, friendly golden labradors had launched themselves on top of us, tails wagging furiously.

"Oh, God," groaned Art, sitting up and trying to fend them off, "oh, *God*—where the hell did they come from?" The dogs kept bounding at us, their big eager faces thrusting into ours.

"It's all right, they won't hurt you!" boomed a voice.

**203**

"That must be the owner," I said. "Dog owners always say that when their mutts have got you pinned to the floor."

"They only want to play!" the voice continued, and a woman in a tweedy jacket strode into view. "They think if you're rolling about on the ground you're going to play with them!" The dogs clambered off us when they heard her voice, sturdy paws digging into our legs.

I started to laugh. It was a crazy interruption. We stood up but neither of us said anything to her as she stalked over to round up her dogs.

"She's surreal," I whispered.

"Don't speak to her," said Art. "She's a hologram. She materializes at the first sign of any sexual activity on the hills. It's her job to stop it."

I laughed. "And if the hounds don't do the trick, she's got a twelve-bore under that jacket. Any more snogging, and we've had it."

"Let's get out of here," Art said, and we headed off down the side of the hill through the trees.

"That was dead rude, leaving without even a word," I said as we left the woods behind us. "We should have asked about her dogs or something. Dog owners like to be asked about their dogs."

"Stuff her dogs. Interfering mongrels!"

We were still giggling as we headed into the village at the foot of the hill and fell in through a pub door. The public bar was nearly empty. Art straightened his face and walked over to the landlord, who was polishing glasses by the till.

"A pint and a half of bitter, please," he said in his deepest voice.

I came up behind him. "*Two* pints," I said. "I'm really thirsty."

"Is she eighteen?" the landlord asked.

"Yes," said Art, as I choked silently behind him. "And two packets of plain crisps, please."

The landlord pushed the two brimming glasses toward us. Art seized one and drank deep. I did the same. It tasted wonderful. I'd got through half a pint before I put the glass back on the bar.

"That'll be four pounds," said the landlord a little sternly. We paid, then headed for the corner of the pub. We curled up in two old oak chairs, knees touching, and started giggling again.

"'Is she eighteen!'" Art said. "What is all this—the Vice Police?"

"Life in the country is supposed to be clean, remember," I said. "We're polluting it with our urban presence."

Art laughed, and said, "Well, I'm glad we are."

"Me, too," I answered.

The tiny lamps were making warm patches of light on the old paneling. "I really like this pub," I said. "D'you want some more crisps?"

Art sighed. "No time. We're going to have to go

soon. It's an hour's walk from here. Can't miss Fran's dinner."

"I wish we could eat here," I said. "Sausages and chips or something."

"I know. But we can't. Look on it as payment for being here. And don't forget to compliment Fran's cooking. Don't just wolf it down like you usually do. I've seen you in action."

I managed to half push him off his chair with my foot, then, laughing, we left.

# NO. 42

It was dark by the time we got back to the cottage. The delicious smell of *coq au vin* washed over us as we stamped off our boots in the hall. I was ravenous.

"Oh, you're back, you two," said Fran as she swept out of the kitchen. "Good. It's ready. Nothing fancy." She swept back.

Ian looked up from his seat by the fire. "Worked up an appetite, have you?" he said, jovially. "Come on, then, you young cannibals. Let's eat."

Before long the four of us were seated around the table, politely handing each other the vegetables, making conversation about the walk we'd had, and Fran's cooking, and whether it was a good idea to build a little conservatory onto the cottage.

"What do you want a conservatory for?" Art asked, piling potatoes onto his plate. "Just walk out the door and you've got all the open space and plant life you could ask for."

"Don't be silly, darling," Fran said. "Honestly, Art,

how many *more* potatoes are you going to take? I don't want open space. I want *enclosed* space."

"So sit in the living room."

She rolled her eyes in despair, and appealed to me. "You know what I mean, don't you, Colette? Somewhere I can look at the sky, but not actually be under it . . . you know, *vulnerable* to it . . ."

"I've got a skylight," I said, brightly.

"Oh, have you, darling? How nice."

"I think," said Art, "that conservatories are bloody horrible. You want the sky—get out under it."

I laughed, and Fran sniffed. "You've had too much to drink, Art," she said. "Ian, he's had too much to drink." Ian picked up the wine bottle and emptied it into his own glass.

"You don't *deserve* to enjoy the sky if you won't get out under it," Art was still saying, and Fran snapped "*Art,* for goodness sake *shut up!*" and I dropped my napkin so I could stick my head below the table for a few minutes and choke.

Huffily, Fran dished up dessert. I remembered Art's rude comments about how I shoveled food down and ate with pantomime slowness. Art started laughing, and Fran got peevish, and pointedly only talked to Ian from then on.

Art tipped himself back in his chair and turned to gaze at the fire. I stared at him, his nose, his jaw, his mouth, the way his hair fell onto his neck, and he looked around, and saw me staring, and smiled.

Then at last it seemed the meal was over, and we were free to go.

"Let's go outside!" said Art. "Under the Big Sky! Let's be *vulnerable* to it!"

"Oh, shut up," said Fran. "Honestly, Colette, I don't know how you stand him."

I thanked her for dinner, and Art and I staggered out, hand in hand. The clean, cold air hit us like water, making us gasp.

We wandered down the slope of the garden. It was pitch black, just the stars showing. The wind was moving the trees, sloughing through the long grass at the edge of the pond. Art put his arm round my shoulders and we walked in silence.

I knew what was going to happen. All through dinner we'd been watching each other. Now there was just emptiness around us. There was nothing to stop us doing—anything. Now it came to it I felt slightly scared.

We stopped at the gate and Art turned toward me, his hand moving to the back of my head. We started to kiss. We were used to each other now. I loved the way I was beginning to know his mouth, its responses, its taste. He was working his fingers into my hair. His other hand moved from my neck. Then after a while it moved lower, across my stomach. I was trembling, a bit. All the times I'd thought about it, and now it was happening. Without quite meaning to, I pulled back slightly.

"You're shaking," he said. "You can't be cold."

"I'm not," I whispered.

We started kissing again. This time I didn't pull back. I willed myself to feel wild, abandoned. And I did begin to feel a little braver. After a while we lay down on the damp grass. I knew we'd reached the stage to move on. It felt very new, being touched like that, and I was too tense to really enjoy it. And I was unsure how to touch him. But we'd moved forward, and I was glad.

After a while I kind of turned away. "I'm getting cold," I lied. "Let's go in, huh?"

Art didn't answer. He lay back on the grass and put his hands behind his head and looked up at the stars for a few moments. Then he stood up and said "Sure," holding out a hand to help me up.

For me this had been enough initiation. I wanted to curl up in bed and think about what had happened.

I wanted to absorb it. Own it.

## NO. 43

We went back through the trees and into the cottage. It was nearly midnight. Ian and Fran were stretched out in front of the fire, swigging brandy.

Art shouted "hi" through the door and Fran airily waved a hand back. They obviously didn't want us in by the fire with them. Which was fine by me.

"Coffee OK?" said Art, as we walked into the kitchen. "Want a biscuit? There won't be anything good—no Jammie Dodgers."

I laughed, and sat down at the old pine table, watching him as he made the coffee. It was really relaxed. I'd wondered if I'd feel shy or awkward with him, but I didn't. I felt very close. Maybe it could all be as passionate and terrific as I'd hoped it would be. I was beginning to . . . trust him. Yes, trust. That was the right word.

We drank the coffee and talked about the cottage, how he'd come here as a kid and loved all the space. After a while we ran out of conversation. There wasn't really a lot to say. He was watching me across the table.

"Art, I'm tired," I said. "Let's turn in. Then we can get up early and go on that other walk you were talking about."

"Sure," he said. "Come on."

He walked into the hallway and headed for the stairs. I pulled my rucksack from underneath the old settle, and followed him.

On the landing, he opened a white-painted door. "This is the bathroom," he said. "It's nice—Fran hasn't got her hands on it yet."

It was very plain: whitewashed walls and a huge old claw-footed bath slap in the middle. I'll sneak in for a nice wallow tomorrow morning, I thought.

Then he opened another door and showed me into a beautiful little bedroom, low ceiling, oak beams, lit by two brass lamps. There was very little furniture, just an old pine chest and a large bed with a terracotta-colored duvet on it.

A large double bed.

Suddenly, with a feeling close to panic, I knew. "This is the only room, isn't it?" I said. "We're supposed to stay here together?"

"Yes," he answered. "It's a very small cottage."

"Oh, God, Art." My voice was cracking.

He put his arms around me. "Oh, come on. Don't tell me you don't want to."

I pulled away.

The same bedroom. Fran had put us in the same bed-room. Art wanted to sleep with me, and they'd said OK.

"So your dad . . . Fran . . ."

"Coll, it's fine. If I bring a girlfriend down, she stays in here with me. They're fine about it."

A Girlfriend. I was A Girlfriend. Fran had made up the bed for us. Putting on a clean duvet cover, plumping up the pillows.

"But they just assumed . . ."

"Forget them. They don't matter. They're probably doing it in front of the fire right now."

I made myself look at him, but I couldn't read any-thing in his face. He suddenly felt like a stranger.

"Coll, it isn't such a big deal. What's your problem?"

"But we haven't . . . we've only just started to . . . to . . ."

"We want to make it together," he said. "It's simple." And he tried to put his arms around me again, but I pushed him away.

"Art, this is—I don't feel right. We don't know each other well enough, not yet. There's still this block between us, this—"

"Coll, the only block between us is sex. The fact that we're not having any. You want us to get to know each other. How can we do that when you're always holding back?"

My mind wouldn't work properly. I felt like someone was pressing the fastforward button. I wasn't in control.

I needed him to understand how I felt. I needed him to stop feeling like a stranger. "Art, I—I can't believe this," I said. "I mean, why did Fran think . . . it's like . . . out of the blue. It's too soon . . ."

He turned away, and walked over to the window. "Too soon for what? You're always pushing me away—not here, not now. When *will* it be right? You want to get married first or something?"

I felt stricken. What a shit. What a shitty thing to say.

Then suddenly something very obvious hit me. "But you knew—you knew all day—all the time we were outside just then—"

"You mean we could have been up here? Yeah, sure. But it's nice making it in the open sometimes."

You shit, I thought. You *liar.* You didn't tell me about the room earlier because you knew I'd have freaked if you had. All that time I felt so close to you, so happy, all that wonderful day—it was a trick. It was a setup.

A kind of horror was rising in me. Everything was slipping away. "Art, you *knew* I didn't expect to sleep with you this weekend," I said, trying to keep my voice steady. "We'd got nowhere near . . . we never even talked about—"

*"Talk!"* He turned back to face me. "What's talking got to do with it? If the feeling's right, you just go with it. You talk too much sometimes, you know that?"

I felt really hurt when he said that. I felt like I was going to start crying. But the anger stopped me.

"And you don't talk at all," I spat.

"I don't know what you mean. What's there to talk about? Come on, Coll. Most kids would think this was paradise. We can fall asleep together afterward."

I looked at the bed. I could feel myself shaking. I'm not getting into that bed just because it's there, I thought. Just because everyone—Fran and Ian as well as Art—assumes I will. Without asking me, without even *thinking* about me and what I want.

"It's too soon," I said at last. "I *can't*."

"So all that writhing about we just did—what was the point of all that? Getting turned on for no reason. It drives me crazy."

For no reason. That time by the pond, that initiation, was "for no reason." Something inside me snapped.

"Well, screw you then! I'm sorry it's been such a drag!"

"*It wasn't a drag!* I just don't see what the big deal is—we've done everything but . . ."

Then he shrugged. And that shrug seemed to say it all. In his eyes, I was a write-off. I could feel the tears pricking my eyes. Oh, shit. It had all gone so wrong. What an idiot I looked. What a bastard he was. He didn't care. I was just one in a long line of girls, only I didn't know enough to play the game properly. Anger and misery exploded inside me.

"You make me *sick!*" I spat, praying my voice wouldn't break. "If you're so desperate for sex, why don't you go and call up one of your ex-girlfriends? Just leave me out of it, OK? Haven't you heard *anything* I've said? You *tricked* me into this! What sort of sex d'you think I'd have after that? I wish I hadn't come here! I wish I was anywhere but here right now. You know what? You're no better than that yob I beat up in the park. It's all on that level for you, isn't it? You make me *sick!*"

Something had slammed shut behind Art's eyes. "Fine," he said. "I'll sleep downstairs."

I wasn't going to stay in that room, not now. "*I'll* go downstairs," I hissed.

Silently, he pulled the huge beautiful duvet off the bed and held it out to me. "There's a couch in the dining room," he said. His voice was ice cold. "Want me to show you?"

"*No!*" I spat, ripped the duvet out of his hands, and ran out of the room. I wasn't going to let him see me crying.

# NO. 44

I staggered downstairs and crept into the dining room. I found the couch in the dark and flung myself down. All my energy was concentrated on crying silently. You blub, I told myself, and I'll *kill* you.

What a bastard. What an arrogant, conniving bastard.

I felt sick with grief. It was over. Everything I'd hoped for had just dissolved. Art wasn't who I thought he was. He didn't care about me, he *couldn't* care about me.

I lay there for ages, staring up at the ceiling, going over it all again and again in my mind. I couldn't stop shaking.

For a while the anger I felt warmed me. Then I began to feel so alone and miserable I ached to be with him. I wrapped myself in the duvet more tightly. You pathetic cow, I lectured myself, where's your pride?

But still a part of me wanted to go up, talk, apologize, *anything*. I couldn't believe everything had fallen apart so completely; I couldn't bear losing him like this. I began to wish I'd just got undressed and got into bed.

So what if I felt in some ways he was still a stranger? I was so gone on him it didn't matter. And that lovely little room—it would have been perfect. Better than the backseat of a car or behind a bus shelter. Better than staying a virgin forever.

Maybe everyone else was right. Maybe all my idealistic views on sex were just an excuse not to do it. Maybe all those years with Mum had made me inhibited and suspicious and anti-men after all.

But I stayed wrapped in the duvet. Something in me wouldn't move, wouldn't creep back upstairs again. What you did was right, I told myself. It wouldn't have worked, like that. Not being tricked into it; rushed into it. It would have been second-rate. Your gut reaction was right. Sex *is* more important than he was making out. It is a big deal.

Then I remembered something Mum had been talking about a few weeks ago. She'd been going on about how sexual standards nowadays weren't much better than those grim old Victorian wedding nights. The leap from kissing to sex in under twenty-four hours. Awful for the girl, she'd said. Women needed to take it slowly.

It cheered me up a bit remembering that now. That was how I felt. I needed to take it slowly. I'd wanted to get used to his body first, and to him touching me. For it to be part of a whole relationship. To go slowly.

Then I started crying again because none of that mattered now because the whole thing was over. He'd blown it; I'd blown it. I'd never be able to even look at him again. Maybe Mum's right, I thought. Maybe she's right about men, after all.

Then I heard giggling outside the dining-room door. I heard a man's voice, very low, and then another little giggle, sort of pleased, knowing. The stairs creaked.

Oh, God. Fran and Ian. I'd forgotten about them. I didn't want them finding out. There was Art, upstairs, alone, and me in the dining room. What would they think? Maybe I could creep upstairs before they woke up and put the duvet back . . . they needn't know. Art wouldn't say anything.

Then I thought—this is crazy. Most kids try to *hide* their sex life from their parents, and here was I planning how to conceal our lack of one. It was almost funny. Except I'd started crying again.

Then the noises started, right over my head. Saturday night noises. No mistaking them. Bedsprings, moans, silence. Creaks, yelps, laughter.

Great, I thought. Rub it in, why don't you. Rub my bloody nose in it. I disappeared even further into the duvet, I rammed my fingers into my ears, but I could still hear the creaking, working into a rhythm now. And finally, low pitched bellowing like a buffalo in pain. Then silence.

In the end, the decision on whether or not to try and hide where I'd slept was taken out of my hands. As the

**219**

night wore on I was sure I'd spend the whole of it awake and crying, and then suddenly someone was ripping open the curtains and letting the hideous sunlight shaft down on me like a spotlight.

And there was Fran, in a pink kimono, with an amazed expression on her face.

"Col—*ette!*" she trilled. "What on earth are you doing in here? Oh, darling—did you have a row or something? Oh, honestly!"

All the misery from last night came flooding back. I blinked up at her numbly, not saying a word.

"I thought I heard raised voices. You should have kicked *him* out, darling. You're the guest. Fancy coming and sleeping down here!"

There was just a tinge of irritation in her voice. I hadn't behaved like a good weekend guest should. I was cluttering up her dining room for a start. Anger flooded into me. I decided I hated her as well as Art.

"Is the bathroom free?" I asked croakily, coldly.

"Yes," she answered. "Ian's gone out for a run. Art won't move for ages. Well, he doesn't usually when he's got someone staying, but then I . . ."

She trailed off as I glared at her. Was it really possible for someone to be that stupid?

It was. "Oh, go and make it up with him, darling," she whittered. "Don't let it spoil today. I want today to be *nice*. Go and take him a cup of tea or something. The last thing I want is him sulking all day . . ."

Ignoring her, I swept out of the room, leaving the duvet on the couch. She'd made up just the *one* bed in the first place, she could clear up the debris. I stomped up the stairs and wrenched open the door to Art's room before my courage could fail me. He was spreadeagled across the bed, face down, still in his clothes. I marched over to my backpack, grabbed it and walked out, slamming the door. Loudly.

Then I dashed into the bathroom and shot the bolt. It felt like sanctuary. I turned the bathtaps on at full blast. I took off all my horrible grass-stained, sleep-stained, grief-stained clothes and rolled them up tight. Then I stepped into the bath, letting the water cover me, letting my hair float out behind me.

As the warmth of the water seeped through to me I wanted to start howling. I wanted to just slip under and drown. But I had to keep control. I had to work out what to do. I felt this tight knot of misery inside me. It felt permanent.

I tried to be glad that I'd found out what Art was like before I slept with him. After a few weeks, I told myself, he'd have dumped you for someone else. That's what he's like.

But the gladness wouldn't come.

I lay there until the water was cold, then I soaped up, shampooed my hair and rinsed off under an ancient spray attachment. The thought of facing Art horrified me. I wondered if I could make a run for it, and spend the day in the woods.

I put on clean clothes, toweled my hair dry, and crept out of the door. Down the stairs I went, no shoes, tiptoeing. Let me escape, I prayed. Just let me get out. I'd reached the bottom when someone sort of rushed at me from behind and got me in a firm hug. It had the effect of an armlock.

"Here she is!" said Ian. "She's been making herself gorgeous, that's all! Breakfast's ready, Colette!" He was propelling me toward the dining room. His words might have been jolly, but his grip was vise-like. I had no choice but to go in.

My dazed eyes took in a vast array of croissants, jams, rolls, fresh figs, and grapes, covering the table. Behind the table was the couch where I'd spent my miserable night. The duvet had gone. All evidence cleared away.

Fran trotted through the door with a dish full of bacon and mushrooms.

"That smells heavenly," gushed Ian. "And I'm ready to do it full justice, my love. I covered five miles this morning!" He sounded really creepy. I hate couples, I thought.

"Is Art up yet?" said Fran sharply. And then, in the doorway, there he was. Hair all over the place, still in yesterday's clothes, looking as though he'd been dragged forcibly out of bed, and glowering horribly. I felt numb. He was like some stranger, wandering in. I didn't know him anymore.

"Fran's gone to a huge amount of trouble to get this together, so let's just enjoy it, shall we?" Ian said urbanely, looking reprovingly over at Art.

And we all had to sit down. It was a nightmare. "Let's pretend nothing's happened" writ large. If Art and I had had a knife fight last night, and were all gory and wounded with bits of us missing, I think we'd still have had to sit there and eat the croissants and drink the coffee and listen to Ian and Fran being happy, as our blood dripped onto the white tablecloth.

"Colette," Ian was saying. "We've mixed up a big jug of Buck's Fizz. Come on, darling. Hair of the dog. We all had a bit too much last night." And he handed me a tall glassful.

Perfect, I thought, alcohol. Obliteration. And if they want me to eat, I'll eat. I'll show that sod he hasn't even put me off my food.

I downed a glass of Buck's Fizz and accepted a croissant, three rashers of bacon, and a pile of mushrooms. I ate them stolidly, full of hate and grief, and I didn't look at Art once. When it was finished, I stood up and helped carry things through to the kitchen. I was throwing off hate vibes like snakes from my skin—little black venomous snakes, spitting rage and sorrow. No one dared come near me.

Then I walked straight out of the house. Ian called after me, "Lunch at two-ish. And don't be late, the Richards are joining us. OK, you two?"

You two. He'd actually said you two. His deliberate obtuseness was almost impressive. It was a Herculean task, ignoring what was happening. They don't care about us at all, I thought, that I'm so unhappy and Art's so grim. They just don't want us mucking up their Sunday Lunch.

I half thought Art might follow, as I walked down the path, and I was ready to blast him if he did. But he didn't.

All I wanted to do was go home. I was longing to climb up into my room and curl up on the bed and bawl my eyes out. I felt like a little girl again, alone and scared, and out of her depth.

I can't really remember how I passed the day. I walked. And I sat and cried. And I slept a bit, curled up in some dryish grass. When I woke and looked at my watch, I realized with dread that I'd have to get back to the cottage. To continue the pretense over lunch.

I wasn't sure I could do it.

# NO. 45

**S**omehow, I got through the rest of that day at the cottage. It was easier during lunch; there were more people, and I could fade into the background. In the Range Rover on the way home I pretended to be asleep. They dropped me off at my gate, and I managed to mutter thank you. Then I let myself in, headed upstairs and lay on the bed and howled, just as I'd promised myself.

No one disturbed me. Maybe no one heard me, tucked away in the attic. As the light faded, I just lay there, silent and exhausted. The terrible thought that life had to go on came over me. Then I went downstairs to make a drink. Mum was sitting at the kitchen table. She took one look at me and said, "Colette—what's happened?"

I collapsed down beside her and started crying again. She patted me, then got up and made me a drink, and when I could get the words out I said, "It's over. We've finished."

"What happened?" she said again, firmly.

I was so glad to tell her—to tell someone. I stared at

the table and mumbled that I'd got Art wrong, that he'd set me up, all three of them had set me up. I mumbled out all the hurt and confusion and grief.

The silence from Mum as I spoke was uncanny. It wasn't like her at all. I risked a look at her face and saw why. She was furious—angrier than I'd ever seen her before. As I watched, she stood up and kind of stormed around the table, swearing as she went. Then she marched to the sideboard and picked up her car keys.

I shot to my feet. "Mum?" I said, in alarm. "What are you doing?"

She turned and looked at me, eyes blazing. "I'm going round there. No one treats you like that."

"You *can't*," I wailed, horrified. "Mum—it's *over!* Just leave it, *please!*"

But she'd walked out of the room, and out of the house. Panicking, I ran after her. "Mum *leave it*!" I screamed. "You can't interfere like this!" I grabbed at her sleeve as she got into the car but she just shook me off. It was like a puff of air trying to halt a great, growing, ocean-born typhoon. In desperation, I ran around the car, yanked open the passenger's door, and got in beside her.

"That's right," she said grimly. "You come, too."

She ground the gears horribly as she shot into motion, driving faster than I've ever known her to drive. Her face from the side looked like some kind of mask. I felt frozen to my seat.

We arrived outside Art's house. Mum wrenched the

handbrake up and heaved herself out of the car. Usually the way the car leaps up on the right-hand side when she exits makes me snigger—it's like the car's heaving a sigh of relief. But this time it didn't. It just made me feel even more lightweight. I got out and followed her to the front door.

I wasn't sure why, but I'd stopped wanting to stop her.

The door was opened almost immediately by Ian. His face lit up into that phony welcoming smile he has. "Colette!" he said, as though I was the person he most wanted to see on his doorstep. "And this must be your mum—we meet at last!" He probably thought we'd come round with a bottle of wine to thank him for a super weekend. His smile pretty soon faded when he took in Mum's expression, though.

"Er . . . come in, both of you! Fran's in the . . . er . . ."

Mum was in, striding toward the light in the conservatory at the back of the house. I followed her. A weird sense of unreality had come over me, as if I were in a dream in which anything could happen.

Ian came along behind, shouting up the stairs as he went, "Art? *Art!* Colette's here with her . . . with her . . . mother."

Fran was curled up on the sofa. She had a glass of wine in one hand, a glossy mag in the other. Jazz played on the CD player. She reared up as we entered, elegant like a swan's neck.

"Mrs. Rowlands! Well, hi! I'm so glad to meet you! Did Colette tell you all about the . . ."

Her voice trailed off. Mum, completely ignoring her, had marched over to the CD player and silenced it. Then she turned around.

"Yes, she did tell me about the weekend. How she hadn't realized that part of the deal was sleeping with your son."

Art had come down, and was standing by his dad at the door. It was so strange, seeing him again. I felt this yearning for him, even now. Fran had risen, a bit shakily, to her feet. They all faced Mum, like a tribunal. But it was Mum in the role of Accuser.

"Part of the deal?" said Ian. "What on earth do you mean?"

"I mean you invite her for the weekend and give her no option but to sleep with him. You make up a double BED for them."

Ian tried to laugh it off. "Oh, come on, now. This *is* the twenty-first century. Art asked her along, we just assumed—"

"You ASSUMED. You didn't ask HER."

"Oh, come *on*. That's up to him. He asks who he wants and he always—"

"Oh, I see," Mum broke in thunderously. "He ALWAYS sleeps with his guests, does he? Well, of course he does. If there's only two bedrooms, his guests don't have a lot of CHOICE, do they?"

"Mrs. Rowlands," started up Fran, in her silvery voice. "Really. We just took it for granted that they . . . that they were sleeping together. Art invited her—it was up to him."

"Up to him. I see. And what other decisions do you leave to this seventeen-year-old BOY?"

"But no one was forced into anything," Fran went on. "Colette slept . . . she decided to . . . she slept downstairs. There WAS no . . . no coercion." And as she said that you could sense the first tricklings of doubt in her mind.

"No COERCION!" roared Mum. "I should bloody well hope there WAS no coercion. But there WAS unhappiness and humiliation. What you did was unforgivable! You put my daughter in a position of intolerable pressure, where she felt she was being weird— FRIGID as your son no doubt told her—if she didn't share a bed with him. And because she had the strength of mind NOT to comply, she had to sleep downstairs on the bloody sofa! What a great weekend! Did she get any breakfast or is that only for girls who play along with your weekend cottage games?!"

Mum paused for breath. She needed it—she was panting. Ian took his chance and cut in quickly.

"Now look here, Mrs. Rowlands. Don't come into my house and start shouting a lot of nonsense about intolerable pressure and playing games. In this family we're relaxed about sex. It's not such a big deal. It's natural, for Christ's sake. It brings *pleasure*." He said the last word with just a tinge of malice, as if he couldn't imagine Mum bringing sexual pleasure to anyone. But she ignored that. She'd got her breath back.

"Well, Mr. Johnson, that is where we differ. I think sex IS a big deal. I think it's very important indeed."

"Oh sure it's important—hey, no one gives it a higher rating than I do." He tried an almost flirtatious laugh. It had all the effect of a party popper at a state funeral. "Of course it's important. There's so much to learn . . ."

Bad comment. All Mum's rage buttons had been pushed at once. "Oh I SEE. So you want him to LEARN about it, ay? Get lots of practice in? It's a sort of extracurricular activity for him, is it? What's the matter, don't they have it on the timetable of that expensive school you send him to? Cricket, badminton, fencing, and SEX? That really IS an omission. You must complain to the headmaster!"

Ian actually took a step backward as Mum bellowed those last words. Then Fran bravely piped up: "But isn't this all a bit over the top? I'm sorry if we were . . . thoughtless. But no one got hurt."

"No one got—!? Oh, but they did. My daughter got hurt. She's hurting now. Luckily she had the courage to say no and get out before she got really hurt. I call being bullied into having sex getting really hurt. But I don't expect you or your son to understand that." Then Mum

**230**

continued, more quietly, "You might have a seaside postcard view of sex—all fun and smut and satisfying basic appetites" (they gawped at that) "but I see sex differently. It involves the emotions and the mind as well as the body. It implies commitment, caring. It's not just romping around and titillation. It's not just PLEASURE." As she spat the last word, she somehow included the whole room in her condemnation. Most of all she included and obliterated the three people standing there in front of her.

There was a silence. The conservatory still seemed to shake with the force of her words.

"I've nothing more to say to you," Mum said. "As far as I'm concerned you've behaved callously, no better than a couple of pimps."

Fran and Ian were too stunned to reply.

Mum began walking to the door. As she passed Art she paused. "I feel sorry for you. You've got very good looks and the sort of pappy, shallow home-life that won't do you any good at all. I'd get out as soon as you can. Stay among these values much longer and you'll end up completely . . . LIMP."

After the topic of the row we'd all had, her last word couldn't have packed more punch. Art recoiled as though he'd been hit. I crept around to Mum's side and went with her to the front door. I felt like a child again, sheltering beside her big safeness. I didn't know what else I was thinking or feeling.

When we got into the car Mum didn't start it up immediately. She looked drained. "OK," she said, flexing her plump hands on the steering wheel. "Tell me you'll never forgive me for doing that. Tell me I'm an interfering old bag. Tell me I'm prudish, riddled with Victorian values, and I just did it 'cos I hate men."

I was silent. Then I said, "I thought you were great, Mum." Because it suddenly flooded into me that that was what I did think.

She let out a long, deep breath. "I need a drink," she said.

## NO. 46

We drove to a quiet little pub and went inside in silence. Mum waved me to an empty table. "Wine, darling?" she asked. I nodded. A bucket full, please, I thought.

Watching her go up to the bar, I felt little pricklings of tears in my eyes. They weren't for Art this time though. They were for her—for the way she'd defended me. Because that's what she'd done. I'd started off ready to die with embarrassment and ended up feeling she was right. She'd stood there, fat and badly dressed, no one's idea of a sex siren, and told those two elegant, designer people that their views on sex were straight off a seaside postcard. She had guts.

I watched as she stood aside to let an old man get to the bar. She exchanged a few words with him and he smiled—he looked warmed. She can have that effect on people. No amount of good dressing and clever haircuts can give off the warmth that my mum can, when she's in the mood. I thought of Fran—perfect Fran—and I felt almost sorry for her.

Mum sailed back to the table with the drinks, and sat down. "Well," she said, "I'm glad you're not angry with me. I had to do it. I had to go round there or I would have COMBUSTED. How DARE they treat you like that? Just assuming you were sleeping together? People like that are—well! You did exactly the right thing. Pity you didn't manage to set fire to their luxury cottage as you left."

We both laughed then, and some of the tension of the last hour slipped away, and the misery I felt lessened its hold on me just a little. "It's not really him I blame," Mum went on. "He just behaved as he'd been taught to. Good-looking kid, hormones pumping round his body, dad egging him on, stepmother making up a double bed for him." She swigged her wine indignantly. "And there with you, my wonderful girl."

I choked on my drink. Wonderful? Me? The most she'd managed in compliments before was telling me my hem was straight.

"Art wasn't going on about me being frigid or anything," I ventured. "He just—he just sees sex differently. But he did try to pressure me. I . . . I really lost my rag with him."

Mum laughed. "Good for you. You keep right on losing your rag with anyone who tries to get you to have sex when you don't want to. Wait until YOU'RE READY." She turned to me. "You're a lovely girl, Colette. I'm proud of you. I want the best for you."

I could hardly speak. There was a big lump in my throat, choking me. She'd never said half—a quarter—of that to me before. Oh, I knew she loved me, but she'd never spoken about pride before, or how she really felt.

"Mum, thank you," I croaked out. "For—for going round there." It was all I could manage.

We both looked down then, and concentrated on our drinks. The moment had passed. But it had happened.

Somehow I had to start getting back to normal. I had to stop crying all the time, and go to school, and come home, and eat, and do homework. I even made myself go to Sonia's class on Monday evening, and the proud little announcement she made about me rescuing Tricia nearly finished me off. They were treating me like a heroine because of what I'd done, but it seemed like nothing now, nothing compared to what I'd been through over the weekend.

Everything I'd hoped for had been smashed, and I wasn't going to see Art again. And I missed him. I missed the Art I thought I was getting to know so much I felt it was slowly killing me.

I analyzed it over and over in my mind. Sometimes I felt angry, and sometimes I felt regret, when I thought, if he'd *told* me there was only one bedroom, if he'd *asked* me, maybe it would have been OK. But then I remembered how he'd been that night, and how he'd set me up, and I felt humiliated, and I hated him.

Mum was very kind to me over this time. She didn't really mention it again, but I knew she understood. And I talked about it all with Val. She was great, too. Not even the slightest undertone of "Well, I told you. I warned you. I said he was spoiled and pushy." Even though she'd been right. Completely right.

She listened and listened, and it helped to hear her tell me he'd behaved like a total bastard, and I'd done the right thing, and I was better off without him. But it didn't take away the grief.

It was over. He'd probably already found someone else.

I didn't go swimming on Thursday. Not that I thought for a moment that Art would be there at the pool, but I just couldn't bear to go back to the place where it had all started. I felt like I'd never go swimming again.

# NO. 47

The week finally finished, and on Saturday morning Val phoned and told me firmly that we were going up to town and she was buying me lunch in McDonald's. When I told Mum, she smiled, and said Val was a good friend to me, and good friends were worth any number of pushy young men. Then she got her purse and thrust a ten-pound note into my hand.

"That's for your burgers," she said. "You go on out and meet Val. I know it doesn't feel like it right now, but you will get over it, Colette. It will hurt less."

Val and I wandered through Top Shop and Gap, all the usual places. I tried to be cheerful but it was hard going. Val kept up a stream of inconsequential chatter, and didn't mention how happy she was with Greg once. She didn't need to—I knew anyway. She sort of glowed with it. Well, that was fine, I was glad for her. All that seemed so long ago now. I didn't want to go back. Greg would never have been right for me.

McDonald's was packed, as usual. You'd think people

who could afford it would eat somewhere else and leave places for us, the needy, to sit at. Val went to join the long queue for food and I hovered, waiting for a table.

Then a family by the window moved, and I grabbed their place. As I sat there gathering up all the leftovers and packaging they'd thoughtfully left behind, a shadow fell over me. Someone was standing outside, staring in. I shoved the tray full of rubbish to the end of the table. Clear off, I thought. I want to be alone with my junk-binge.

But the shape didn't move, so I finally looked up.

It was Art, looking through the window at me.

Every part of his face was vivid to me.

I watched him turn away. I watched him come through the door, walk over, and stand opposite me. The air around me seemed to be shaking slightly, as though I was sitting somewhere at the beginning of an earthquake.

"Coll," he said, his voice hoarse. "Colette. Look, I must . . . I need to talk to you. We can't just leave it."

I did something like a flap with my hand that he took as an invitation to sit down. I couldn't look at him, I didn't trust my face. *Talk?* What on earth was there to talk about?

"I just wanted . . . I wanted to say I'm sorry. About what happened. I behaved like a real shit. It's just, I wanted you so bad I—"

"Oh, spare me," I muttered. "You set me up."

"Coll, I didn't. It wasn't like that."

**238**

"Yes, it was."

"Look, when Fran said bring you along to the cottage, I was—I was going to tell you. About the rooms. I mean, I was going to talk to you about it. Only I—"

"—never got around to it."

"I thought it would be OK. I thought you wanted to, I really did. I mean, we were getting there—we'd got a lot more—"

"What the *hell* difference does that make?" I said.

"Well—"

"You should have *asked* me."

"I know. I know I should. Only it's not that easy to . . . I thought it would just kind of happen. I mean, what was I supposed to say? 'Fancy a shag this weekend, Coll?' If I'd just *told* you about the room, you wouldn't have come, would you?"

*"I don't know."*

He looked straight at me when I said that. Deep inside, I'd started to shake. But I kept my face like a mask.

There was a silence. Then Art said, "It was so strong between us. I mean, the way you kissed and everything . . . just the way we *were*. I couldn't understand why you kept—"

"Why I kept *what?*"

"Well, pushing me off. I thought maybe if the place was right; I thought you'd just go along with it, when you saw the room. I—I thought it would just happen."

"And when it didn't you thought you'd turn on the pressure and—"

"OK, OK. I know. I was a shit. A complete shit. And now I've blown it with you. And—and I really wanted it to work."

From the corner of my eye, I saw Val turn from the counter with a laden tray and start toward us. I sent out psychic rays so strong I'm surprised she wasn't thrown backward by their force: *Not now. Not now. Go away. Go away.* She stopped with a start when she saw Art sitting there and then—*oh Val, thank you!*—she wandered off to a different table, as if she often came in on her own and ordered two Quarterpounders all by herself.

"Say something," Art muttered. "Anything." He was fumbling with an old napkin on the table. I'd never seen him this untogether. It was . . . to be honest, it was wonderful.

I remained silent.

He sighed, and said, "That was some scene, when your mum came round. God, I was scared. We had one hell of a blowup afterward. Dad was slagging off your mum. Fran got upset and shouted at me and said she admired your mum for looking after you. Then Dad laid into her and she burst into tears and left, then he started to pull his 'men together' routine with me, and I told him where to go."

I glanced up and said, "Good."

He laughed then. "Look, I don't like the way they

are any more than you do." There was a pause. Then he said: "You know, if you hadn't blown up like that, we could've sorted it out. I mean, it was just a *room*. We could've just slept there."

That got me. "You think back over what you threw at me that night," I snapped, "and you say again that we could've just *slept* there. You behaved like a *pig*. We'd had a fantastic day, and I felt so *close* to you, and then I find out you'd *lied*"—I leaned across the table toward him—"and then you come out with all that crap about it's no big deal and what's my problem. You say I talk too much—"

"I never said that—"

"Well, you've had some kind of communications *bypass*. Things don't just *happen*. Sometimes you have to *discuss* them. You know—*relate*. I mean, I had no idea what you thought about me, even. Not really. I felt like just someone in a long line for you—a really long line."

"You weren't, Coll. You *aren't*. I didn't know what *you* felt, that's why I . . . I . . . ." There was a silence, then he said, "Come on, you know what's between us. You must know how I feel."

I took a deep, shaky breath and closed my eyes so he couldn't see into them. Then I glanced over at Val, sitting a couple of tables away. She was chewing her way through her second burger, pausing now and then for a swig of Coke from one of the two huge paper cups in front of her. I love you, Val, I thought. What a mate. No

241

complaints, no criticisms, not even a sly "So you're talking to him now?" look. You just cleared off and let this happen.

Then I turned back to Art. "You know, if you'd managed to say *any* of this before, that . . . that *scene* would never've happened. You're like some kind of weird *prude*. It's like you can't talk about what you feel, or . . . or sex. Do it all you can, but don't talk about it, because that's too embarrassing. Don't you grin at me like that. You are, you're prudish."

"OK, OK, I'm prudish. I'm a total prude. But you didn't talk about it either, Coll."

"Oh, yes, I did. A bit. Anyway, I wasn't the one going off like an express train."

"Give me another chance. Please."

"It won't work, Art."

He reached over the table, and got hold of my hand.

"It will work," he said. *"Please."*

# NO. 48

I didn't go straight home after that. I just took off and walked. Inside me, the energy was so strong, I had to do something.

I wasn't stupid. I knew that one miraculous conversation in a McDonald's doesn't change everything. Real transformations don't happen that quickly. I knew we weren't going to walk into any sunset together, all our problems solved. But perhaps we'd got something to build on, now. Something honest.

And all I could think of was Art's face, his face across the table, and how good it had felt when he'd got hold of my hand.

When I got home I went straight into the kitchen. I was starving—well, Val had eaten all my lunch. "Mum," I called. "Mum? I'm going to get myself a sandwich, OK? I won't be in to eat later—I'm meeting Art."

Here it comes, I thought, as Mum swept into the kitchen, the doorframe trembling as she passed. "ART?" she said.

"Yes. I met him in town today. We had a long talk. He apologized for what happened."

"REALLY?"

"Yes, really. He *really* apologized. We had a *really* great talk. And I'm going to meet him again."

She stood there looking at me, smiling. Wait for it. She's just letting the rage and derision build up behind that smiling front, then she's going to let me have it . . .

"Good for you," she said.

I was too astounded to speak.

"Pick your jaw up," she said. "I have complete faith in you, Colette. You've got your head screwed on and you know your own mind—you've proved that. You go out and have fun with your-young-man. Just keep him in order. Don't stand for any more nonsense. Keep on letting him know who's boss."

I found my voice. "No one's going to be boss, Mum. We're equals. I want an equal relationship."

"An equal relationship, eh? And they say idealism is dead in the young! Well, I'm delighted to hear it. Just make sure *he* knows it's equal, too, all right?" And she left the room, smiling.

She always gets the last word.

This time, I didn't mind.

# Author's Glossary

**binbag** garbage bag.

**blitzer** an intense and destructive event. From Blitz—the night-time bombing of Britain by the Germans in World War II.

**carrier bag** shopping bag.

**chivvy** to nag at, to hurry along.

**chuffed** delighted, pleased.

**cock-up** mess.

**cop off with** make out, maybe start dating.

**crease you up** make you laugh (so your face creases).

**daft** silly.

**DMs** Doc Martens.

**duff** bad, useless.

**Durex** a brand of condom.

**flash** classy, impressive.

**fruity** sexually excited.

**fug** stale, suffocating fog.

**gap year** a blissful year off, often used for traveling, between school and college.

**get off with** make out, maybe start dating.

**git** from illiGITimate. Like bastard, only milder—can even be affectionate.

**gobsmacked** astonished. Gob = mouth, so like you'd been hit in the mouth.

**grafted** worked hard.

**grotty** nasty, unattractive. From "grotesque."

**half-term** a week off school halfway through each term.

**hod** an open wooden box on a pole, for carrying bricks on a building site.

**hoovered** vacuumed.

**hunk features** a hunk is an attractive male. This is Val's mocking name for Art.

**J-cloth** a type of disposable dishcloth.

**jive** swing dance.

**jumper** sweater.

**lose your rag** lose your temper, go mad.

**Marmite-pot** Marmite is a traditional, black, yeasty spread for bread, and it comes in a round jar. So round, deep black eyes.

**National Front** a small British political party of the far right with racist views and often thuggish members.

**Netball** a girls' game, like basketball.

**pappy** worthless, with no substance.

**paste** thump repeatedly.

**petting chart** Coll made this up. Similar to first base, second base—a way of showing "how far you went" sexually.

**pinny** apron.

**pitch** field.

**ponso** an affected, vain man.

**poxy** nasty, rotten. Pox = syphilis.

**prat** idiot, loser.

**public school type** in England, "public" schools, illogically, are the ones you pay for. Val is not keen on "public school types"—she thinks they're arrogant, overprivileged, and lacking in broad social experience.

**pulled** made out with.

**ratted** drunk.

**sarnies** sandwiches.

**scarper** to escape at top speed.

**shag** have sex with. This can be jokey or insulting, depending on the way it's said.

**Sharon** a girl with not much brain and lots of makeup.

**shattered** exhausted.

**slag** slut.

**slag off** to be rude and insulting about.

**Smarties** M&Ms.

**smoothy** suave, envy-making.

**snog** heavy-duty kissing.

**sod** obnoxious person.

**sod off!** go away!

**Swiss cheese plant** *(Monstera deliciosa)* a houseplant with leathery leaves that has holes in it like Swiss cheese.

**swot** someone who studies hard. Always derogatory!

**take the piss out of** to mock, to tease.

**tanked up** drunk.

**tatty** scruffy, worn out.

**topping yourself** killing yourself.

**tracksuit** sweats.

**try** touchdown in rugby.

**twee** overly sweet.

**twigged** realized.

**wanker** a complete idiot (wank = masturbate).

**whacked on** talked relentlessly.

**Wimpy bar** like McDonald's. JUST like McDonald's.

**yob** an aggressive, uncouth young man. Yob = boy spelled backward.

# A note about the

## English educational system:

English kids feel very over-examined. At age 16, they take about eight GCSEs (General Certificate of Secondary Education) in subjects such as math, French, and history. Then they can leave school or—if their grades are good enough—go on and do three or four A (Advanced) levels in their best subjects. Coll's mum made her stay on at her school to take her A levels, but the trend nowadays is for kids to leave and go to a sixth-form or tertiary college, where there's a bit more freedom. After that, when they're 18, they probably take a "gap year," then go on to university or college to get a degree.